# The Lost Treasure of Nostradamus

# The Lost Treasure of Nostradamus

## A Mary Thresher Adventure

By *Jonathan Lee Miller*

AKA

## Mark Lee Masters

**To order additional copies of this book, contact:**
Xlibris Corporation
1-888-795-4274
www.Xlibris.com
Orders@Xlibris.com
84759

# Table of Contents

# Acknowledgements

My teachers must be thanked for their patient work with me during the many years of schooling I took as preparation for being a writer. I thank my parents for all the support they gave me down through the years. Thanks be to God for giving me enough years of mental clarity to write many books, even though I didn't write my first novel till I was fifty years old. I must acknowledge the help of many readers who have encouraged me by showing enthusiasm for my books. Without such people, it is more difficult to write. Last of all, I thank my patient wife, who helps me have an organized life which is conducive to writing. Her love and help cannot be praised too highly.

Any resemblance of characters in this book, to people in real life, is purely coincidental. I have the highest respect for the people of Kingston, Jamaica and the people of the entire country. The beauty of the island and its people is why I often write about this area of the world.

I am a sincere Christian and wish to denounce the use of black magic. Nostradamus is believed by some scholars to have used black magic and astrology to make his predictions. It is my greatest wish that all my readers stay away from black magic. I wish that all readers would love Jesus and his teachings as I do. My complete loyalty goes to the Lord God, Jehovah, Father of Jesus Christ, and to his Son. It is my belief, in spite of being an enthusiastic Christian, that authors are at liberty to draw from all of creation for their subject matter, in the interest of creating a captivating story.

The Latin writings of Nostradamus, which have been included in this book, are in actuality completely fictitious concoctions of my own making. Nostradamus would role over in his grave if he could see my feeble attempts at imitating his flowing elegant Latin style of writing.

Please do not see the inclusion of séances in this book, as an invitation to engage in such activities. I am only trying to add to the suspense of the story with my description of the séances. If you attend séances, it is my personal opinion that you are quenching the Holy Spirit within you, if you had it in the first place. Dabbling in the occult, is not fruitful in helping you mature as a Christian. This is all the pedantic preaching I intend to do during the writing of this book. I only hope that it is enough to assure everyone that I am not a witch. I don't ever want to be a witch, and I don't think it is good for other people to be witches. It is my honest hope, that reading about my imagined séances, will not harm anyone in the least.

I feel, out of fairness to Nostradamus, I should explain that I actually have no way of knowing if he currently resides in hell with Satan. I wrote him into the story because of his notoriety. I thought he would add interest to the story. During my readings about his life, I found that as a physician he did much to heal plague victims during his time. He was smart enough not to bleed them repeatedly, as most other doctors of the time did. He used red rose petals to cure with. I personally believe he would have used occult sayings or prayers as well, though of what type I can only guess.

He was exceedingly well educated and generous with the poor. He liked the Catholic faith, although he was born Jewish. He could not believe in his own salvation. I personally speculate that such a belief may have been related to the intense guilt he must have felt when his wife and children died while under his medical care.

# Chapter One

# The Search Begins

The wind was savagely gusting and the towering waves were whipping their white caps more violently against Mary's hundred foot long salvage boat. The boat, named Deep Diver, was tossing from bow to stern. She was pointed to the east, facing the heart of the approaching storm. Mary's dive partner, Bill Phillips, was in the water hanging on to the salvage net as it cleared the water. Mary was twenty years old, with long red hair, and was a slender terribly attractive woman. Her green eyes seemed to glow as she smiled to see the approaching treasure. Bill was a handsome tall man of twenty, with black hair and a neatly trimmed moustache. His tanned skin made him look quite attractive. He was an Irishman with some German ancestors in his background, as well. The net was filled with gold and silver ingots. Bill passed his tanks up to Mary and then deftly scrambled up the dive ladder on the stern of the boat.

A powerful cruiser pulled up to the port side and three men dressed in worn out jeans and white T-shirts jumped aboard. They were the Jamaican gang who had been following the salvage boat for several weeks. Two of them rushed Bill, as one pointed a large shark knife at Mary to keep her at bay. Bill lunged aside and threw a karate kick into the nearest man's groin. The man fell groaning to the deck. The other man, a bigger tall man with a scar across his right cheek, drew his shark knife and jumped at Bill. Bill caught the wrist of the knife hand and used his other hand to force down on the back of the man's hand. The knife fell to the deck. Mary pulled a throwing knife from its sheath on her back and threw the knife, with uncanny skill, into her assailant's heart. He staggered back with a stunned look on his face. Crimson blood oozed out around the knife as the man fell to the deck.

Bill jammed his knee into the tall man's groin. When the man bent over in pain, Bill chopped him in the neck with a lightning quick karate chop. The man fell heavily to the deck. The powerful cruiser roared loudly as it surged forward. The rest of the gang raced back towards Kinston Bay. The storm was closing in on everyone.

Mary and Bill tied up the two living men and pulled the treasure on board. They hoisted anchor and Bill steered the boat back towards Kinston Bay. The Jamaican shore line was now difficult to see, as the rain started to pelt down viciously and the wind spiked the waves up. As Mary Thresher stood beside Bill, sweating with perspiration from the excitement, she allowed herself to relax a bit. There was a long five mile trip though immense waves, ahead for them. She finally sat down and lapsed into reverie about the times during which she had known Bill.

She had met Bill while she was walking along the marina at Montego Bay. He had just brought his seventy-five foot yacht over from Fort Meyers, Florida and was waxing the outer cabin. Mary had stopped to make a little small talk. She liked his nice tan and his dapper moustache. She wondered right away what it would feel like to kiss a man with a moustache, but she played it cool. Mary had total recall for their times together. Those times started to unfold again for her. She had said, "What's your name? I'm Mary Thresher. I'm in the yacht at the far western end of this marina." Bill responded, "I'm Bill Phillips. I just arrived from Fort Meyers. Nice to meet you." Mary explained, "I always take a walk past all the piers each day. I get to meet new people and get my exercise." Bill offered, "Can I get you a drink? All that exercise must work up a thirst!" Mary replied, "I could use some orange juice. No alcohol please. I don't need any of that." Bill responded, "Coming right up." He disappeared into the galley and returned quickly with her drink. He said, "I don't use much alcohol either. I only have a beer or two at bed time, to help me relax." Mary replied, "You should give it up. It hardens the arteries and ushers in a premature death." Bill laughed, "I suppose you're right. I know it isn't good for my health. Possibly you could help me relax in the evening." Mary laughed, "You were quick with that one! I like quick wits in a man. Can I help you wax your cabin? I have strong hands and I give lots of attention to detail." Bill smiled, "I could use some help. Owning a boat is quite a bit of work." Mary laughed, "Tell me about it. I'm always cleaning my boat. The teak needs plenty of attention. I don't want it to start looking bad." They worked on the boat for hours as they got to know each other.

Mary asked, "Where did you get the money for this thing. It's almost new!" Bill chuckled, "I'm related to the people who make these boats. They gave me this one as a demo. All I have to do is talk it up to people over here and keep it clean." Mary asked, "Do they pay for the gas too?" Bill said, "I'm not as wealthy as my relatives, but gas prices don't bother me. I've been raking in money for the last five years, on blackjack. I've got a system that always works. My dad used to drive me around from casino to casino. I wore makeup to make me look older and I had false I.D.s. Now I'm invested in Chinese and European high risk stocks. I'm also invested in United States steel companies. They're paying off well. I don't mind a little risk."

Mary exclaimed, "That sounds impressive. I want to hear about that blackjack system some day. My father gave me my yacht for my eighteenth birthday. He lives near Kingston. I'll tell you about my father later. Have you read any Ian Fleming?" Bill smiled, "He's my favorite author. I have all his books." I have the James Bond movies too. I love watching them. Would you like to watch one with me now? We've done enough waxing for one day." Mary answered, "I'd like to watch *From Russia with Love*. It's one of my favorites."

They went to the aft cabin and started watching the movie on a giant flat screen LCD television screen. The lights were low and they held hands gently as they watched the movie and ate pop corn. When Bill stopped the movie to make more pop corn and get drinks, Mary asked some questions she'd been mulling over. "Bill. I think you're a really great person. You're a great host! I think I should tell you something about me, so you don't get disappointed later." Bill asked, "You aren't lesbian, are you?" Mary laughed, "I assure you. I'm not lesbian. All my dreams are about men. It would be great if we could start seeing more of each other, but I want you to know about my father, first. He's real old fashioned. He's offering to let me keep my yacht as a gift, and he's going to give me his entire estate, if I'll keep my virginity till I'm married. Does that sound too atrocious?" Bill explained, "I am disappointed, to say the least. This yacht is basically designed as one large seduction machine. It has a cozy steam sauna with surround sound, there's a hot tub and a massaging king sized bed. All that stuff will be going to waste, now." Mary explained, "Dad said I must stay a virgin. He didn't say I couldn't have fun." Bill responded, "I'm glad you warned me, so I won't get my hopes up for too much. Let's just play it by ear. I like spontaneity. I don't like to plan everything out." Mary sighed, "You're right. I try to verbalize everything. Let's just watch the movie."

When the movie started getting romantic, so did they. They put the movie on hold and kissed passionately for a long time. Finally, Mary pulled back from Bill and said, "You'll like my dad. He's got a great sense of humor. He wants me to live a full life. No babies right away. He doesn't believe in abortion." Bill responded, "I don't either. Your dad sounds quite logical. If you don't want babies, don't make them. I can live with that." Shall we finish the movie?" Mary frowned, "No. Let's watch it tomorrow night. You're not busy are you?" Bill laughed, "I'll never be too busy for you."

Bill said, "I think it's time for the hot tub." Mary stated, There's something else I need to tell you." Bill grimaced, "Not more confessions. What else won't your father let you do?" Mary laughed, "No. It's nothing like that. You see I'm looking for a partner. Not a marriage partner. No, I need someone to go treasure hunting with. I've been planning this for some time. Will you let me lead you on a treasure hunt?" Bill laughed, "I'd follow you anywhere. No, really. I love adventure. What sort of treasure do you have in mind?" Mary explained, "I'll tell you in the hot tub." The each got dressed for the hot tub. Mary always wore a swim suit under her clothes when she was around the marina. They held each other tenderly in the hot tub. The water was giving off steam and felt delectably warm.

Mary asked, "Do you scuba dive?" Bill assured her, "I'm an excellent diver. I've been doing it since I could crawl." Mary explained, "I'm quite experienced as well. I'm also a black belt in karate. Do you have martial arts training?" Bill said, "I've been training in karate since I was five years old. I have a black belt too. Why does that matter with treasure hunting?" Mary explained, "I'm expecting that we'll need to fight to keep our treasures. In Caribbean waters, gangs of modern pirates keep an eye on treasure hunting boats. They like to move in at the right moment and steal the prize. I've heard about it happing more than once." Bill said, "They'll be in for a surprise if they try to take anything from us."

Mary was rudely brought back from her reverie by a rogue wave which jostled the boat with unusual viciousness. After the shock of that temporary threat to the boat, she fell back into her deep state of reminiscence.

Mary had played footsy with Bill as she went on with her plans. "I've got some maps I'd like you to study with me tonight. I also have a few important books which I've been studying. I'll show you the important passages. They speak of unsurpassed riches to be found under the sea. The books are by Michel Nostradamus. In his last writings to his son, he mentioned his hidden writings on treasure. He wrote to his son, in Latin, about the location of an engraved copper page of writing which would lead to riches. The writing was in elegant Latin, although it is said he originally wrote it in French." Bill asked, "What was the profession of Nostradamus?" Mary answered, "He was King Henry II's physician and an oracle. Some of his prophecies, which were written in quatrains, came true. Most of his prophecies didn't come true. He mixed astrological and mathematical calculations, with black magic to come up with his prophecies. His prophecies, which weren't in quatrains, never came true. That's why I only study the quatrains. The quatrains to his son were written in 1555. I've just about figured out where the copper page is hidden. It has something to do with his telescope. Do you know Latin?" Bill laughed, "Sure I know Latin. I studied it for several years in high school. I liked it so much, that I've been taking courses in it over the internet. Maybe I can help you understand the verses Nostradamus wrote to his son. I can't wait. Let's go see your books." Mary frowned, "You're tired of being in the hot tub with me?" Bill said, "We can come back here later. First things first. You've got my curiosity piqued. I must see those books." The smile came back to Mary's face. "Let's go. More of this later."

They got their street clothes back on and walked briskly over to Mary's yacht. Mary's yacht was bigger than Bill's. She apologized, "I'm embarrassed about how big this thing is. It's a hundred and twenty feet long. My dad has more money than he knows what to do with. My mom died when I was three. He's always been real close to me because of that. She died of a mysterious jungle fever. When they first moved to Kingston, the mosquitoes were still bad. Now they spray for them. Dad's parents were sugar plantation owners. Dad's quite patriotic. He gives money to help disabled veterans. He loves making more money all the time. I get a little bored with that, myself." Bill quipped, "I love more and more money. I think your dad and I will get along fine."

Mary took Bill to the galley. They made some more coffee. It was midnight. They carried their coffee with them, as Mary led Bill to the yacht's library. The library was full to the ceiling with ancient books. On a table in the middle of the room, were the books Mary had been studying on Nostradamus. She pointed out the beginning of the quatrains about the earthly riches. As Bill read, Mary watched his eyes. He was intense and eager. His wit was apparent. In no time at all, he had read the pages related to the hidden treasures.

Mary explained, "Nostradamus had read much writing about creating pure silver and gold from other elements. He decided that such writings were nonproductive. Nostradamus flamboyantly described burning those writings, and how they flamed up with Satanic fury. He was highlighting the evil nature of such endeavors. He wanted his son to stay away from that sort of pursuit." Bill stated, "He doesn't tell where the treasure is. He only makes reference to his copper telescope case. He calls it the home of the eye. "Pagina del cuprum esse intra de domestica del oculus." Quite literally translated, he says, "The page of copper is inside the home of the eye." His telescope was his eye on the universe. I'd say he hid the location of the treasure in his telescope case." Mary exclaimed, "You're a total genius. I've been studying this book for a year, and I thought the secret copper page was stored inside the telescope. Now we're getting closer. Before his death, Nostradamus gave the telescope to his son. The son was loyal to his father and preserved the writings about treasure, even though he wasn't interested in the treasure. He was a devout Christian who found his father's notoriety a little disturbing. Future generations of Nostradamus had their patriarch's love of writing. They couldn't help but mention the telescope and the hidden message. In the middle sixteen hundreds, the writings of Nostradamus came under criticism from the Catholic Church. The family members who wrote about the treasure, started writing in mirror images to prevent people from deciphering their writings." Bill asked, "How did you find out all this?" Mary answered, "My father's hobby is Nostradamus. He reads everything he can find about him. That's how I found out about him. My dad wants me to find the treasure. Since the treasure was mentioned in quatrains, dad thinks Nostradamus was under true inspiration when he wrote about it. The treasure originally belonged to the King of France. Nostradamus had seen the treasure. He spoke of a large chest containing it. He didn't mention individual items, but he wrote that the treasure was one of the largest concentrations of wealth in the world. His visions told him that one day it would become lost at sea. Dad wants that telescope, or the case. Whatever contains the location of the treasure."

Bill asked, "Why is your dad so eager for more wealth? He already appears to be more than just a little wealthy." Mary explained, "It's the challenge of it. He feels the treasure is waiting for the one who can find the telescope. He wants the telescope and case. He wants the message. He's obsessed with Nostradamus. So am I. It's the main thing my dad and I talk about. I just learned, from some newly discovered books, that the telescope was shipped to a family winter house in Jamaica, back in 1824. The ship sank during a hurricane, just before it reached Kingston Bay. It's in deep water, somewhere about five miles southeast of Kingston. The storm had blown it south of Kingston. It was spotted by a fishing trawler that narrowly escaped the storm. The Nostradamus family has always kept immaculate records. We're lucky there! I think we can find that ship. It hasn't been looked for yet, because there was no shipment of precious metals on board. The telescope and case were being shipped with a cargo of wheat and cloth. I feel the hidden message will still be intact. Nostradamus was clever enough to inscribe his most important documents on thin copper plates, so they would last indefinitely. He was a terribly clever man who thought about the future, all his life."

Bill asked, "How will we find a ship, when all we know is that it's five miles out. That leaves many square miles of ocean to search. It could take decades to find the ship." Mary asked, "Would that be too long for you to spend with me?" Bill laughed, "I don't mean that. I love diving. I'll dive all my life, anyway. I suppose searching for a telescope and case is as good as anything to do. I love seeing the fish and the underwater seascape." Mary went on, "My dad has access to side scanning submersible metal scanners. They will speed our search immeasurably. The telescope ship was a French merchant ship. It was heavily armed with cannons. Our metal detectors will locate the cannons. The cannons will be near the ship." Bill exclaimed, "Now that sounds good. I don't mean to sound greedy, but how will we split the riches?" Mary looked into Bill's eyes. "You'll get plenty of money. I'll ask my dad to write up a contract. I promise we won't cheat you." Bill went on, "I trust you. We have quite a bit in common. I think we'll be spending many years together. We can spend the money together. We can continue diving, just for the fun of it."

Mary took Bill's hand, "I think I'd like to see the rest of that James Bond movie now." They returned to Bill's yacht and made some more pop corn and coffee. As Bond worked his way past one danger after another, Bill and Mary struggled to preserve her most valuable asset, her virginity. They managed well.

In the morning, Mary called her father and asked him to rent them a salvage vessel at Kingston Bay. She told him about the new book she had just read which divulged the location of the ship carrying the telescope and case. Her dad's name was James Thresher. He was a tall man with short red hair and a clean shave. His face was freckled like Mary's. He was delighted to hear of the progress on finding the riches of Nostradamus. It impressed him that Bill was able to help with the Latin translations and could read Latin so rapidly. He asked his daughter, "Where did you find this new friend of yours?" Mary replied, "I was taking my usual walk along the marina, when I saw him waxing his yacht. He was nice looking and looked industrious, so I thought I'd take a chance and introduce myself. I think he's wonderful. I can't believe what great luck I'm having."

Once again a monster wave rocked the salvage boat. Mary was exhausted from the ordeal she was going through. In no time she fell back into a near sleeping state of reverie. She could practically see her father's face as he spoke to her concerning Bill.

"How soon can you and Bill be here?" Mary answered, "We'll take the next plane we can catch. We should be there tonight sometime. I'll call you when we're most of the way there. You can meet us at the airport." Jim said, "I'll be there. We can have a bonfire on the beach tonight. I'll get it ready." Mary added, "Don't forget the marshmallows, chocolate bars and graham crackers. I love the smorz. Have some milk there too." Jim retorted, "Don't worry about a thing. I'm an old hand at this. You know that! Remember to call me. It's a half hour drive to the airport. I don't want to be late. Have a good day now. Goodbye." He hung up suddenly, like he always did. He hated long goodbyes.

Mary went to the cabin and woke Bill. She spoke softly, "Bill, honey, my dad wants to meet you. He's having a bonfire for us. Will you come with me today to Kingston?" Bill stretched his arms and yawned loudly, "Certainly, my sweet. Did you tell him you're still a virgin?" Mary frowned, "He knows. I wouldn't have been so happy sounding if I had disappointed him." Bill asked, "When do we leave?" Mary answered, "We'd better pack right away. I'll get us the earliest flight I can book. He's meeting us at the airport."

In no time they were approaching Kingston. Mary called her dad, so he'd start driving to meet them. He was there waiting for them when they entered the airport. Jim shook Bill's hand, "Mary says good things about you. Your knowledge of Latin is commendable." Bill humbly acknowledged, "I'm quick with languages. It runs in the family." Mary said, "He found an interesting detail in the letter of Nostradamus to his son. I'll tell you on the way home." They climbed in the car and headed west along the coastline. Mary explained, "Bill found that the copper page revealing the location of great wealth isn't in the telescope. It's hidden in the telescope case. Of course we'll no doubt find them together." "Yes," exclaimed Jim, "that will be of great help. It would have been a pity to destroy that wonderful telescope, looking for something which wasn't actually inside it."

They pulled up to a low slung but large bamboo bungalow, with many large out buildings. A big three stall garage was attached to the bungalow.

On the nearby beach, Jim already had a large bonfire burning. It was almost dark. They went to the bonfire, where Jim had everything prepared. They cooked marshmallows and made smorz, a sandwich of chocolate and cooked marshmallows between graham crackers. Jim asked Bill many questions about his life. They were getting along wonderfully. When darkness came, Jim pointed out the constellations of stars above them. It was like a dream, star gazing on the beach with the sound of the waves in one's ears. Bill was glad he had come here.

Finally they went back to the bungalow. It was elegantly appointed within. There were expensive paintings and sculptures in the living room. The floors were done in white marble. Bill asked, "How do you protect all this. Don't you have trouble with intruders?" Jim laughed, "I have a large kennel full of German Shepherds. I keep a full time trainer here. He doubles as a body guard. I have an excellent cook and several grounds maintenance people. They're all armed and know how to deal with trouble makers."

Jim led them into his library. It was similar to Mary's library. It was full of books on Nostradamus. There were also ancient maps of the oceans. A giant internally lighted glass globe of the earth was stationed in the center of the library. The tasteful use of color, made it a delight to the eye. It glowed with deep reds, blues and shades of purple. Jim said, "I spend many hours here studying and translating. It's my favorite room." There were several reclining chairs around the room, with beautiful oriental lamps of cut colored glass, beside them. The lamp shades portrayed scenes from ancient China.

Jim stated, "I've hired the salvage boat for the two of you. Do you need any protection?" Mary jumped in, "We can take care of ourselves. We don't need a bunch of body guards watching over us." Jim continued, "Just offering. This is a rough town. You can't be too careful." Bill reassured him, "We'll keep our eyes open. We'll call you if we see more trouble than we can handle." Jim said, "Be sure to do that. I'll be available if you need me." They all had some herbal tea and then went to bed.

In the morning Jim took them to the marina and showed them the rental car he had arranged for them. Next they went to the salvage boat. "She's all loaded and ready to go." Jim explained. "It has G.P.S. and radar. The boat's range is five hundred miles." He helped them load their suit cases onto the boat and then took them grocery shopping in the city. When they had plenty of supplies loaded on board, they launched the boat and headed out for deep water to the southeast.

The first day out, they scanned with their metal detecting side scanners for ten hours. Bill steered the salvage vessel while Mary watched the monitors closely. They had started at a point far to the north. They were certain the ship was south of them. They were working systematically to the south, covering about fifty yards of ocean on each pass. They could only go about ten knots per hour. The hours seemed long and the work would have been boring if it weren't for the conversation. They were covering an area that was ten miles long from east to west. They used the boat's G.P.S. system to keep the boat on course. Every three hours, they stopped for a break. That was when they did the most talking and playing. They limited their breaks to thirty minutes. Their first break gave them time for some much longed for kissing. They had been watching each other with interest, as much as their duties had allowed them to. They had started the day at six in the morning. At nine o'clock, they stopped for their first break. Mary stated, "Well, not a single beep on the sonar. I didn't think we'd find the cannons immediately. We certainly don't want to miss them, though. It would be terrible if we had to start all over again." Bill responded, "I like your determination. We need to stay professional at this. We mustn't be distracted by our hormonal urges!" He laughed and grabbed her for a long hug and some passionate kissing. They both loved kissing, and skipped their breakfast so they could kiss longer. After thirty minutes they dutifully went back to work. When their next break came, they were quite hungry and spent their time eating and drinking. By the end of the day they had made almost twenty passes, and moved over one half mile to the south. The sonar had been perfectly silent.

Bill wanted to spend some hours kissing and being passionate, but Mary discouraged him. She said, "We'll need our energy for these long weeks of work. This isn't a honeymoon! I need to know more about you, Bill. What are your parent's names and what are they like?" Bill smiled, "You're right we have lots of things to talk about. My dad's name is Pete Phillips and my mom is Jessica Phillips. Dad spends all his time investing money in the stock market. He's a day trader. He's brilliant at it. Mom keeps records for him and spends lots of time gardening. She loves raising her own food and growing roses. They own a farm near Orlando, Florida. They rent out most of it to orange growers, but mom uses about ten acres for her yard and garden." They went on talking about each other's families for hours. After supper they watched some television together and then went to bed early. They wore light black silk pajamas and snuggled up to each other in the roomy bed at the bow of the Deep Diver.

Mary whispered, "I'm glad I know you better now. I promise to be more romantic after we get our work further along. I don't want you to think I'm too easy or anything like that. I like you more than any guy I've ever dated. You really know how to kiss. I bet you've dated many beautiful women, haven't you?" Bill evaded, "They weren't nearly as beautiful as you, but yes, I have dated many women. I love to be with a woman. I try not to spend too much time alone. This job is pushing us together quickly. It's almost like we're married. I think I'd like to go steady at least, if that isn't too old fashioned." Mary smiled, "I'd love to go steady with you. I think we're getting along great. There's more to you than just a hot set of lips!" Bill replied, "Thanks, Mary. We have much in common. I think we're meant for each other. I am used to going a little faster with women. You're not just another woman, so I'll try to be patient." Mary stated, "My father would be proud of you. Now let's try to get some sleep. Don't feel my body while I'm sleeping. I need my sleep. Just put your hand on my hip. Now go to sleep." "Yes, dear." said Bill, feeling like he was already married. Bill asked, "Most couples lose much of their passion after a few years of marriage. Would you promise to keep me satisfied till the day I died?" Mary asked, "Is this a marriage proposal?" Bill said, "No, it's just a question. I don't want to get too close to a woman who will be saying no all the time when I ask for sex." Mary turned and looked at him by the light of the night light. "Read my lips, Bill. Yes, yes, yes. I will always say yes. The energy of a horny man is to be used properly. You will always be exciting to me." Bill said, "Thanks, Mary. I was worried about that. The fact that you can wait for sex, made me worry that possibly you aren't heavily endowed with desire. You could be faking some of your passion." Mary explained, "I long for you. I'm telling you the honest truth. When the time comes, when it feels right, then I'll give you as much passion as my dad will allow. He wants me to have fun. I'm sure he wants you to be happy with me. I just need to act like a lady and not be too fast. I need for you to respect me and feel lucky to have me. You know what you mean." Bill replied, "I know just what you mean. I'll wait as long as I need to. You should compromise a little, though." Mary asked, "What do you mean?" Bill explained, "After this, we kiss and hug as much as I want to during the evening, after the work is done." Mary laughed, "If it won't tire you out too much, I promise." Bill sighed and laid back on his pillow. He placed his hand on Mary's hip and they went to sleep.

At five in the morning, their alarm went off. They took turns using the shower, and made themselves a quick breakfast of marmalade toast and eggs. There was plenty of milk in the refrigerator. They each had a glass full and then got dressed for work. Bill watched with interest as Mary got dressed. She said, "Don't get any ideas, Bill. I trust you or I wouldn't be dressing in front of you." Bill stated, "You can't blame me for looking. You are an attractive woman after all." He walked over and helped her fasten her bra. She thanked him and finished dressing. They started their routine. Day after day they searched and searched for the cannons.

After two weeks of searching, they found the cannons they were looking for. The ship was close by. It was only in one hundred and fifty feet of water. Jim went down several times with the boats salvage basket. He was lucky enough to find some gold and silver bars from another ship that had broken up nearby. He loaded them into the salvage net and followed it back to the surface. He would find the telescope later. The ingots were too good to pass up. He might not be able to find them later. Bill tugged on the rope signaling Mary to bring up the net. He held on to the net and let it pull him back to the surface. Mary's mind skipped quickly over the fight with the Jamaican gang and she found herself awake once more. She stood beside Bill as he steered the boat through the fifteen foot waves. They could barely see any trace of the shoreline.

Now that Mary's dream like trance had brought her full circle back to the present, she felt renewed and more confident. Things would go according to plan, she felt. Mary stated, "I think we may need a little help from my dad, after all. Some of his security personnel would make me feel better about this project." Bill responded, "I agree completely. We've proved we can do well on our own, but it would be nice to be able to concentrate more on the diving, and less on fighting pirates." Mary laughed, "That's a certainty! My dad won't think any less of us for asking for help. He knows we aren't afraid. It's only being practical. He'll insist on coming along, though. He won't be a bother. He'll spend all his time in the cabin working on his computer. He has his entire Nostradamus collection in his laptop. He spends most of his time studying those books. He loves studying in a darkened room with only a few black candles for light. He's always talking to Nostradamus. It's as though he really thinks he's talking with the man. I don't think my dad's a witch, but those black candles make a weird impression. All his staff are a little frightened of him. Jamaican's tend to be a little superstitious anyway. The black candles and talking to someone who's dead makes them a little nervous, to say the least."

Bill smiled, "Many wealthy people become eccentric. They don't need to try to fit in, like most people. Independence becomes a way of life.

Possibly he is talking to Nostradamus. That doesn't mean he isn't one hell of a great businessman. You can't argue with that much money. He's doing something exceedingly right!" Mary frowned, "I worry about him. That much money can get a person into serious trouble." Bill replied, "With his money, he can get himself out of quite a bit of trouble. I don't think you need to worry about him. I like him. He's terribly intelligent. Anyone who's as fluent in Latin as he is, has his share of gray matter." Mary said, "He was impressed with your Latin translating ability. With both of you helping me, I should find the copper plates of Nostradamus, with no trouble at all." Bill responded, "I'm going to do my best to help. It's not just the money. It's the challenge and the curiosity. What type of treasure could Nostradamus possibly have known about?

Their salvage vessel finally reached Kingston Bay. As soon as they docked, the police were there to take away the pirates. Mary had phoned them on the way back to the bay. A detective took Mary and Bill's statements. They weren't detained. Mary's dad was friends with the Chief of Police.

Once they were done answering questions, Mary drove Bill to her dad's bungalow. Jim met them at the door. "You must have run into some trouble other than just the storm," stated Jim. Bill asked, "How did you know. Did Nostradamus tell you?" Jim laughed, "I see Mary's been filling you in on all my secrets. I talk to Nostradamus, but he doesn't concern himself with current events much. I keep asking him more about his hidden riches. He just says over and over, 'The copper plate will tell the story. Find the copper plate.' He loves mystery. I guess he doesn't want to spoil the fun of treasure hunting."

Mary asked, "Is fighting with pirates fun?" Jim replied, "It will give you some stories to tell your children about. I hope there weren't too many of them." Bill said, "We killed one and tied up two more. The others took off after they saw us overpower the first three." Jim said, "Good job. Those pirates need to learn to leave people alone."

They talked over the excitement with the pirates and caught up on each other's current lives. They snacked out of the refrigerator as they talked at the kitchen table. Gallons of hot strong coffee were consumed. Jim wanted to know every detail of Bill's life. Bill also was full of questions for Jim about his life and work. Before they knew it, the clock over the refrigerator said 12:02 A.M.

Jim changed the subject, "Mary's old enough now, and you already know I speak to Nostradamus, would you like to see if he'll make his presence known with the two of you present?" Bill smiled, "I've been to séances before. Still, I'm curious. What does Nostradamus do when he appears?" Jim laughed, "He speaks in formal Latin. He loves to impress." Jim went to the kitchen and poured them all some orange juice. He led them to the library and motioned them over to his reading table. It was a small round oak table, about four feet in diameter. He instructed, "You can set your drinks on the small end table next to the round table. I need the round table to be clear for now." He went to his roll top desk at the north end of the library and opened the bottom right drawer. From it, he lifted a black table cloth. Carefully he spread it out over the round table. The cloth was embroidered with a large white pentagram. It covered nearly half of the table.

Next Jim returned to his desk and removed five brass saucers from the drawer. He placed them on the five points of the pentagram. Finally, he returned to the ornately carved mahogany desk to gather up five thick black candles from the top right drawer. He placed them on top of the brass saucers. He carefully lit each candle with his butane lighter which was made of solid gold and was decorated with tiny branches of red coral. Jim invited Bill and his daughter to sit at the table. He closed the blinds at all the windows. They faced east and south. The library was at the eastern end of the bungalow. The windows opened onto a well manicured lawn which was bordered, two hundred yards away, by dense jungle growth of hardwood trees and vines. As he closed the blinds, Jim remarked, "There's an exquisite full moon tonight. I especially love to contact Nostradamus when there's a full moon. It puts me in the mood for the supernatural."

Jim turned off the electric lights and walked to the round table. He carefully took his seat at the table. "Nostradamus is usually quite eager to speak to me. His existence is quite boring. It is an afterlife in limbo, they call it. He isn't quite in hell, yet he isn't in heaven either. Satan was pleased that Nostradamus had made prophecies which were inspired by delving into black magic. Therefore, Satan spared him from the usual tortures of hell. Yet, despising all humans as Satan does, he relegated Nostradamus to an eternity of boredom, only to be relieved briefly by occasional visits from people such as me." Jim drank a small glass of ganga extract which had been prepared for him by his grounds keeper, who was a witch doctor. It helped him tune into the spirit world.

"Nostradamus was a physician to the King of France in the middle fifteen hundreds, as I'm sure Mary has told you. He is used to speaking before an audience. I don't think the presence of a couple of my friends will bother him. Stretch your hands out across the table and we'll form a circle with our arms and bodies. This is just something I cooked up. It adds to the intrigue, don't you think?" He laughed mischievously. Bill replied, "Whatever you say, Jim. It's your séance." Jim smiled and tried to look relaxed. He continued, "I should have had George bring enough ganga extract for you two as well. I'll call him." They dropped hands and he dialed his cell phone and spoke to George. "I want my guests to experience the séance more the way I do. Would you bring over two more servings of ganga extract?"

In about ten minutes, George appeared at the library door with the drinks. He was a muscular dark tan man with black hair and a moustache. There were red tattoos of snakes on his arms. He wore no shirt. His hairless chest was decorated with a light green dragon which was breathing orange and red fire. When he turned to leave, it could be seen that the rear half of the dragon was spread over his right shoulder and down his back. There was a slight oriental appearance to his eyes, even though he looked like a Latin American for the most part. He could have had relatives from Mexico or Costa Rica. He left as quickly as he had arrived, without saying a word.

Jim stated, "He's an excellent witch doctor. He can cure snake bite and many types of fever. He has potions that produce visions and potions that help you sleep. The ganga is his favorite. He is constantly drinking it himself. He says it helps him stay in touch with the spirit world. It also relaxes him. He informs me that he tends to be a little too high strung. He used to be a pirate, when he was younger. He's been working for me for the past fifteen years. I pay him enough that he doesn't need to engage in illegal activities anymore. He's quite loyal to me. I couldn't ask for a better grounds man and body guard."

Jim noticed that Mary's and Bill's eyes had narrowed and were a little blood shot. Their pupils were dilated. He said, "Take my hands now. We'll start the séance. The ganga has had time to work. Now I'll call on Nostradamus." He paused in silence with his eyes closed. When he reopened his eyes, there was a slight greenish glow to them. He said, "Nostradamus, I feel your spirit within me. Speak now, and let us hear the wisdom which you hold so dear." Jim's voice became a deep and coarse whisper as he channeled for Nostradamus. "Who have you brought with you tonight? Always before, you came alone." Mary spoke, "I am Jim's daughter, Mary. My good friend Bill is with me. We are loyal to Jim. You can speak freely." Nostradamus whispered softly, "It cheers me to hear young voices. You must remember my words. Things are often not as they seem. Loss can actually be gain. Don't waste too much time grieving your father's death, when it comes. He's only . . ."

Jim's voice quickly turned back to normal. "That blasted spirit! They always want to predict death! How uncreative! He doesn't scare me!" Jim stormed out of the library. Bill asked Mary, "What was that all about?" Mary replied, "Jim wanted Nostradamus to hint about the treasure. It would appear that Nostradamus was telling us something which my dad doesn't want us to know about. We'll never find out. Dad is secretive about many things. He never tells me where he's going or what he's doing. He loves his secret life!" Bill replied, "Well, at least we know he actually does speak to Nostradamus." "Yes," stated Mary, "but I don't think we'll be invited to listen again soon. My dad won't give him another chance to tell too much."

Mary led Bill out into the south yard and suggested, "We can walk along the beach in the moonlight. I love to hear the waves at night." Bill responded, "That should be relaxing. Lead the way." Mary led him across the yard and onto the beach. They stood together, holding hands and watching the moonlit waves cascading softly onto the sandy beach. There was a magnificent chorus of tree frogs singing to them from the edge of the forest. They walked along the beach towards the east so as to come closer to the jungle, and hear the frogs better. Mary stopped in her tracks, about fifty feet short of the jungle's edge. "We should stop here. The mosquitoes are bad further down the beach. Dad has his men spray for them, near the house. Where they don't spray, the mosquitoes will carry you away." They stood for a long time and listened to the frogs. "Wait here," whispered Mary. She ran to the house and returned with a blanket. She spread it out on the sand, as close to the water as possible while still being safe from the waves.

She coyly spread herself out on the blanket like a graceful cat. Bill sat down beside her and looked down into her wide green eyes. He could see in her eyes that she was in a playful mood. He tickled her ribs mercilessly. When she had writhed about and giggled enough to suit him, he deftly unsnapped the front of her pants and rolled her over on her stomach. Mary laughed, "What are you doing." "Back rub time," stated Bill. He did his best to give her a professional massage as he spoke softly to her, "Do you think your father was really as upset as he acted, about what Nostradamus said?" Mary replied, "I think he was. I don't see what bothered him so." Jim added, "Yes, it seemed as though Nostradamus was just muttering platitudes about death and grief. There does indeed seem to be more here than meets the eye." Mary explained, "If there was something we need to know, dad would tell us about it. I think we should act like nothing happened, and let dad take the lead."

Bill stopped rubbing her back and lay down beside her. They drew closer till their bodies were tight up against each other. Bill kissed Mary's lips. She kissed him back with equal enthusiasm. It was nearly dawn before they were completely sated and fell apart from each other, exhausted and looking up at the late night stars. They walked hand in hand back to the house for some sleep.

Several thousand miles north of them, in an Indiana casino, an interesting event was taking place. In a deluxe suite at the Blue Chip Casino, in Michigan City, the two top executives of Imperial Petroleum were having an off the record meeting with no minutes being taken. Imperial Petroleum C.E.O, Derrick Sanders, was briefing his vice president, Warren Miller, about a top secret operation. Mr. Sanders was six feet tall, fifty-five years old, with all white hair. He was slim and fit, with muscular arms. His eyes were deep set and sinister, with heavy bushy white eyebrows.

Mr. Miller was black haired and also had sinister looking eyes. His nose was sharply pointed, and caused him to look somewhat like an angry ostrich. He was slightly heavy for his frame, and was sweating profusely with worry about the meeting. Mr. Sanders said, "If word of the operation gets out, Miller, our gooses are cooked. I'm only going out on a limb like this, because our entire fortunes are at stake. I've had listening devices installed on Jim Thresher's house and on his daughter's yacht. Any man who owns the majority of our stock, and is as meddlesome as he is, needs to be watched carefully. He loves big profits, but he has too many scruples. He's a super patriot. Always crying about 'the good of the people.' If he gets in our way, you know what to do."

Mr. Miller nodded in agreement and responded, "We're both after the same thing here, Mr. Sanders. I haven't worked my butt off all these years, just to let some billionaire scuttle my profits right when they're getting good." "Precisely!" shouted Mr. Sanders. Then he whispered, "I want you to have a crack team of professionals on standby, to eliminate Thresher and his daughter. They're on to something big. That new boyfriend of hers is a problem too. Get all of them. If you botch this, I'll hang you out to dry!" Miller responded, "No mistakes. I know four of the best . . ." Sanders stopped him, "I don't want details. Just get it done. If you miss any one of them, we'll be investigated. I'll deny any knowledge of this plan." Miller defended himself, "I haven't gotten where I am by making mistakes. Leave it all to me. We won't be suspected. It'll look like the work of pirates."

Sanders continued, "If Jim Thresher is this excited about a copper plate which tells of great treasure, it must be something incredible. Billionaires don't get excited about an old cannon or a small pile of sunken ship's treasure. Our bonuses and commissions are nothing compared to what Thresher is after. We'll let them locate the ship and then eliminate them. With him out of the way, we'll have the treasure and we can run this company the way we want to."

Miller asked, "Do you have their salvage boat bugged?" Sanders assured him, "My people are working on it tonight. We'll have spotters on the shore mapping their dive locations. I don't trust too much high technology. They might find a G.P.S. signaling device. I'm having the listening devices installed by the best in the business. It's unlikely they will be discovered."

# Chapter Two

## Planning the next dive

Dawn broke through the night with the sound of tree frogs and locusts. Golden rays of sun created a light show of illuminated fog amongst the trees in the yard at Jim's house. He was up early, as was his custom, trimming one of his favorite small trees. It was a six foot tall Tamukyama Japanese Maple. Jim was encouraging the tree to take on a more spread out umbrella like appearance, as was typical of the species.

He paused and slowly scanned the yard, admiring the twinkling of golden light on the dew drops which trickled down along the long blades of grass in the yard. He whistled happily to himself as he mused over how much Mary seemed to like Bill. To Jim, Bill seemed like a fun loving happy person who would be good for Mary. He had worried about her getting too close to him in such a short time. He knew Bill was a gentleman and wouldn't push Mary to lose her virginity. Jim knew his own thinking was conservative by the modern standards in some circles. He wanted his girl to be happy. Early babies weren't what he thought was best for Mary.

He laughed to himself as he thought about how tired the late night passion had made Bill and Mary. It occurred to him that they would probably like to sleep in late. Jim had seen Mary getting the blanket. It was the same blanket he and his wife, Jeanie, had always used for their star gazing on the beach.

Jim missed his wife as much as when she had first died, seventeen years ago. He was only able to keep going on, because he loved his beautiful adopted country of Jamaica. He loved his Nostradamus studies and he loved Mary. He knew he would never remarry. His thoughts were too caught up with Jeanie. He often saw her at his séances. The séances were an every night ritual for him. He was completely enchanted with them. Jim was not a Satan worshipper. He just needed to see his wife and consult with Nostradamus. Jim knew he was not on solid Christian spiritual ground. He wanted to eventually give up the séances and become a better practicing Christian.

Jim's father had been a staunch Baptist, and was strongly against séances and dabbling in the occult. Jim had rebelled against his father's fundamentalist beliefs, thinking it would be better if he could think things through for himself. His father, David, had died at the age of seventy when a hurricane capsized his yacht off the northern shore of Jamaica, near Oracabeza. Jim felt a little guilty about how he had argued so much with his father about religion. He knew his father was right, but he just couldn't give up the séances, yet.

Jim snipped off another low branch from the trunk of his Tamukyama tree. He spoke softly to himself, "They will never forget these times they're experiencing now. People's first times together are etched permanently in their brains. The passion and intensity of the initial encounters causes total recall." He thought some more about Jeanie, when they first found love, there on the secluded Jamaican beach, under the stars.

She had come to Kingston to visit her parents, who had purchased a large sugar cane plantation. She had been studying at Purdue University, in Indiana, to become a forester. She loved trees, and wanted to be a timber buyer. Jim had met Jeanie as she was examining the forests near his home. Jim's parents were living in Kingston, at the time, and had left their forest home to him. Jeanie fell quickly for Jim. She could see how much he loved the forest. They had their love of trees in common. They also both loved boating.

Jim stopped in his thoughts and cursed a mosquito which landed on his hand. He called George Gonzalez, his head grounds keeper, on the cell phone. George was an early riser too, and was making his morning coffee. Jim said, "George, you'll need to spray the mosquitoes again today." George answered, "I'll get right on it Mr. Thresher. I know how much you hate mosquitoes!" Mosquitoes were responsible for the death of Jeanie. Jim never tired of killing them.

Jim went to the house and entered the kitchen. He made some instant Folgers coffee and had a piece of marmalade toast. Then he woke up Bill and Mary. He didn't want them to miss the beautiful sunrise, even though he knew they would be longing for a little more sleep. Bill was in the guest bedroom. He woke quickly to Jim's knock on the door. He got dressed and went to the kitchen. The toast was popping up as he entered. Mary was already at the table having her first slice of marmalade toast. Bill still had lip stick all over his face, from kissing Mary. She laughed and washed it off for him. Jim said, "It must have been a wonderful time on the beach last night. Did you see any interesting constellations?" Bill chuckled and replied, "Your daughter taught me all about them. She's a real astronomer. She knows quite a bit about astrology too. She told me you've helped her find out about it from the readings on Nostradamus." Jim stated, "I was more interested in the prophecies of Nostradamus than in astrology. One cannot learn all about Nostradamus without coming into contact with much astrology. The man was totally engrossed in it. He also used black magic to help him go into trances and conduct séances. His readings in magic go back to the fourth century A.D. Because of pressure from the Catholic Church, he found it necessary to say his prophecies were from God.

Bill said, "I'd like for both of you to come to the basement for a little while. I have some special wine in the cellar which I would like you to taste." They followed him to the wine cellar. It was locked with a heavy padlock. Jim opened it and turned on the light. They entered the large room full of hundreds of bottles of fine wine in racks. Jim said, "You can sit at the table with me for a little while. I'm sure this room isn't bugged. You can't be too careful when planning your next moves. I need to tell both of you some things which I need to be sure are kept secret. I've found listening devices in this house before. King Henry II was always eager to hear the prophecies of Nostradamus, no matter where they actually were inspired from. The king thought so highly of Nostradamus, that he allowed him to view his largest and most beloved chest full of treasure. It was the impressive sight of all that treasure which inspired Nostradamus to search the spirit world for information about the future of the treasure. Although, there is no mention of it in the writings of Nostradamus, I'm certain the king would have asked him to investigate what would happen to his treasure. Nostradamus learned from his occult searching, that the treasure would be lost at sea. He even named the approximate location where the treasure would come to rest. He couldn't name the location in a book, or the treasure would become available to any loathsome gold digger. He wanted the treasure to be found by someone of high intellect and strong desire. He didn't make it easy. He wrote the location on a copper plate. I'm sure Mary has told you about it. The plate is thin and small. It is inscribed in Latin. Mary told me you were able to discern that the plate is located in the telescope case and not in the telescope. Our books told us the approximate location of the ship which carried the telescope. The telescope ship is what you were near when you brought up the silver ingots and were interrupted by the pirates. Please, Bill, no more silver ingots. I want the telescope!" Bill assured him, "Yes, Jim, I'll try to stay focused on our mission."

Jim whispered, "The French Kings were partial to precious gems of the highest quality and rarity. I'm sure the treasure has some of the world's most impressive gems with it. There are no doubt large quantities of golden art work as well. We can concern ourselves with other ship treasures later. This treasure of King Henry II is most likely one of the most valuable treasures located anywhere in the world. There will be others looking for it soon. There are smart crooks in the world, who watch everything people like us are doing. They are just like the pirates who attacked you yesterday. They want to get things the easy way. We need to be more clever than they are. At this point, I would say that having enough security personnel, and moving quickly, are the main ingredients of cleverness. I'm bringing in another boat for the security people to live on. They will take turns maintaining a presence on Deep Diver. We must be ready tomorrow to head back out to the telescope ship. Once we find the copper plate, we will still need to decipher it and then search out the treasure. Nostradamus is rooting for us. He told me once that Henry II is being tortured by Satan, and has no concern whatsoever about his lost treasure. We can go back upstairs now. Don't mention anything about the extra security or that we know we're being listened in on and plan on moving quickly to the telescope ship."

They went upstairs and all agreed to go for a walk on the beach. They walked a long time and discussed the details of the next day's dive. Jim stated as they walked, "Although I'm coming along with you, I'm leaving everything up to the two of you. This is your search. I'm only going to be working with the security team. I'll spend most of my time going through my lap top and reviewing my information on Nostadamus and the treasure. I want to be sure we aren't missing anything important." Mary replied, "Thanks for trusting us with something this important, dad. I know the treasure means quite a bit to you. We won't let you down."

Bill said, "I can't stand being in the house when I know it's full of listening devices. Isn't there something we can do?" Jim explained, "I'm having a specialist over here this evening to clear the devices from the house. It will alert our enemies that we're on to them, but I can't stand having the bugs in the house either. I'm doubling security at the house, to prevent anything like this from happening again. We can drive into Kingston for a noon meal and do some shopping for the dive. We'll need a few more groceries. That will help pass the time until my security people can be gathered together. You can both stay on the boat tonight if you like. My grounds keepers will come along to serve as security. I always take George Gonzalez with me. He serves as medicine man as well as head grounds keeper. You met him yesterday at the séance." Bill responded, "I'd like that. The boat won't be bugged will it?" Jim answered, "Anything is possible. We need to stop speaking out loud about our plans. If we must discuss things, we'll need to make noise or loud music which will fill the bugs with sound so they can't hear us whispering. Do you understand?" Bill said, "Sure. That makes sense. We'll operate under the assumption that there are bugs on the boat. That only makes sense."

Bill and Mary packed quickly and Jim drove them to Kingston. George went with them. They purchased the essentials for the voyage and had dinner at Lobster Grande. It was a sea side restaurant which featured sea food and fine wines. The restaurant was open to the public, but the prices dictated that mostly the well to do of Kingston and tourists with deep pockets frequented the establishment. The restaurant had a nice hill top view of the ocean. It was on the far eastern edge of the town, right in the middle of a grove of tall palm trees.

They were escorted to a table at a large window overlooking the ocean. It was a windy day and the waves were six feet high. There was a large deck outside the window. A young couple was out there feeding dinner rolls to the seagulls. The gulls were noisily crying out as they swooped down to snatch up the food which was thrown into the air for them.

Jim's party all ordered the lobster dinner. Jim selected a dry white wine from the wine list. It was a German wine called Swartz Katz. Jim said, "Mary and I always have some Swartz Katz when we're together. I'll stop by the liquor store after our meal and get a couple cases to take on the voyage." Mary commented, "That will add some cheer to the voyage. We must get plenty of cheese to go with it." Bill said, "It sounds like we'll be sailing in style. I can't wait to get into the water and find the telescope." Jim cautioned, "Remember to speak softly. We don't want to be overheard. Of course our enemy already knows we're after the telescope. They just don't know what the treasure is."

The wine arrived before the meal. After the waiter offered Jim the cork to smell, he poured a small portion in Jim's glass. After sniffing the glass with pleasure, Jim stated, "We'll have this bottle now. Bring us another bottle to go with the meal, if you will." The waiter responded, "But of course. The meal will be ready shortly." He poured each of them a glass of wine, bowed slightly and walked briskly away. Bill said, "The waiter certainly is well trained. I wonder how they get such good help?" Mary responded, "The tips here are excellent. I think that's why the waiters strive so hard for excellence." Jim added, "Well put, Mary. You get what you pay for. Part of the reason I come here, is the excellent service. The food is top notch as well."

When Mary had savored the first third of her glass of wine, she started grinning slightly. She said, "This wine always makes me smile. Why does it do that?" Bill responded, "It is so dry, I think it tightens certain muscles in the cheeks." Mary continued, "It makes me feel happy though. Why is that?" "It's possibly a paired response. When your brain experiences that you are smiling, there is a feeling of well being. It's purely Pavlovian." explained Bill. Mary said, "I'm glad you're with us, Bill. Your analytical brain will certainly prove useful." "At your disposal." quipped Bill.

"What did you think of our little séance?" asked Jim. Bill responded, "It was the best one I've been to. It's amazing that Nostradamus can speak through you. I'd like to hear more from him. Is it possible he would appear and speak, so you could ask him some questions? I'd like to learn more about the spirit world." Jim assured him, "We can have another séance tonight. George was just telling me that he feels we can listen in on Nostradamus without his knowledge. A double dose of the ganga extract will make us as sensitive as gods. If we long to listen in, it will happen, George says. He has learned much from just listening silently. Nostradamus has told me of his occasional conversations with Satan. He is proud to be one of the few humans which Satan communicates with. If we could listen in on such a meeting, it would be truly enlightening."

Bill asked, "Is it possible that too much ganga may hinder our search for the telescope case?" Bill laughed, "I'm so used to it, it doesn't hamper me a bit. It's a little like being an alcoholic. They can drive quite well, even with a level of alcohol in them which would make other people have a wreck. Mary's quite used to the stuff. I've been letting her use it since she was a young girl. I felt it would increase her sensitivity to the supernatural." Bill explained, "It made me feel a little dizzy at first. I know I'll get used to it. I feel strongly that I'd like to listen in on Nostradamus and his conversations with Satan. That would be a truly unique experience." Mary laughed, "We can try many times if we need to. I find the feeling which the ganga gives me, to be quite pleasurable, whether we communicate with Nostradamus or not." Bill asked George, "How do you make the extract?" George whispered, "It a secret process. You must promise not to tell other people."

Bill replied, "You can count on me." George continued, "I boil the ganga weed in water. I keep boiling it till the water is mostly gone. I drain off the water and put it in a bottle with a cork. It's an easy process. Most of the local people just smoke the ganga weed in cigars. That's hard on the lungs though. If you use the ganga every night that way, you get lung problems and serious coughing spells. The extract is the best way to go. It also gives a quicker and more strong experience, which is necessary when you want to speak or listen to the spirits."

Bill asked, "Do you ever use the ganga just to get high?" George frowned, "I use it for spiritual work. Nothing more. The tourists and lots of the locals use it that way. Not me. I'm a serious witch doctor. I don't want to anger the spirits by playing in foolish ways with the sacred weed."

The lobster came and they all settled into eating and drinking more of the delicious wine. The home made bread was wonderful. They spread it with real butter. Jim asked the waiter to bring another loaf. They dipped the lobster in small bowls of real melted butter. George looked like a gentleman in his white suit and hat. They had all dressed up for the dinner.

As soon as they had finished their meal, they went directly to the salvage vessel. Deep Diver had been fueled by the marina, and was ready to set out to sea. Jim's body guards were on another boat moored next to Deep Diver. Jim explained, "As I mentioned yesterday, I'll have a couple of the guards stay on Deep Diver with you. The other eight guards and I will stay on the security vessel. It's called The Gull. We'll load our things now and set off immediately. There's no point in wasting any time."

They all loaded their suit cases. Mary steered the boat quickly out to sea. The Gull followed close behind. Mary allowed the G.P.S. system to map out their course for getting back to the sunken French ship. As she steered she asked Jim, "When will we have the next séance?" Jim smiled, "I was planning it for tonight. All the boat's gear is in order. We'll have plenty of time for a séance before we hit the sack." Mary sighed, "I was hoping we'd get to do that tonight. You've really got my curiosity up about what we might be able to listen in on. I never thought I might get an opportunity to spy on Satan. This won't get us into some kind of trouble will it?" Jim responded, "As long as we're all quiet and don't say anything, I don't see how we can get in trouble for just being sensitive and listening to the spirit world. It isn't like we're trying to do something to hinder Satan. I'm sure he has better things to do than to attack people who just want to listen to him." Mary asked, "Why don't you go get the galley ready. That would be a good place to have the séance. It will be dark in a couple hours. We spent quite a bit of time at the restaurant. I'd like to find the ship, set anchor and do the séance, so we can get to bed early." Jim stated, "Good thinking. I'll go to the galley and set things up right away. George and I will mix up the ganga drinks and cool them in the refrigerator." Jim and George went below deck to the galley. Jim spread out his pentagram cloth on the table and dug the candles and brass bowls out of his suitcase. George explained, "The drinks, they taste better if we use fruit juice. What kind we got?" Jim opened the refrigerator. "We've got papaya and orange juice." George said, "That's good. We can use both." He opened one of his large bottles of ganga and poured a double dose into each of three glasses. Jim stated, "You can pour yourself one to, George. We'd like you to join us tonight. It should be quite interesting." George smiled, "I don't mind if I do, Jim. I usually don't like to get too close to the devil. But like you say, if we keep quiet and just listen, what could be the harm in that? I always say prayers to Satan when I work my cures, but I never spied on him. I knew I probably could, but I haven't been that adventurous yet. They say that Satan doesn't like anybody. Even those that are loyal to him. It doesn't pay to try to get too friendly with him. I keep it all business. I just say my chants and hope for the best. I know he likes the burning of the ganga. It's his favorite thing. I usually burn some as incense when I'm working a cure." George added the orange and papaya juices and placed the glasses in the refrigerator.

Jim and George went back topside when the drinks were in the frig. They talked about witchcraft, as Mary guided them steadily to their destination. In a couple hours they were at their destination. Jim and Bill lowered the anchor. The sun was just starting to set. The wind had died down and the sea was rather calm. Gulls were calling out and begging for food. George stated, "It's good luck to feed these birds. I'll get some bread from the galley." He disappeared below deck and came back in a minute with a loaf of bread. They all had fun feeding the gulls and watching them swoop down for each morsel that was tossed up in the air. When it got dark, they went below deck and had a round of bacon and eggs before the séance. The bacon filled the entire galley with its delicious odor. Once they had finished cleaning the dishes, they sat down for the séance.

# Chapter Three

## Jim's Nautical Séance

Jim asked George to set the ganga drinks on the table. Jim lit his candles around the pentagram which he had draped over a table in the middle of the galley of Deep Diver. Then he turned off the electric lights. They each drank their ganga fruit drink. Holding hands in a circle around the table, they waited for the drug to take effect. They quickly went into trances which allowed them to listen in on a curious dialogue between Satan and Nostradamus. No other humans had ever been able to listen in on Satan without his knowledge. The ganga was powerful indeed, to be able to make Jim and his party, so sensitive that they could spy on the master of evil. Jim, Mary, Bill and George, all kept perfectly quiet as they heard the initial words of the evil one.

Satan: I am truly bored today. It is the same as with millions of days which I have experienced. Of all the people in my realm, one man stands out as more interesting than the rest. I must call on Nostradamus. He is a wretched human, but I am driven to distraction by my boredom. Refined intelligent angels will not come near me for pleasant conversation. I must stoop to conversing with a mere mortal. This is my plight. What else can I do? Nostradamus! Where are you? Come quickly. I require your presence at once!

Nostradamus came into the presence of Satan and spoke briefly.

Nostradamus: It is I. Nostradamus. Why have you called me? Do you wish to torment me? Nostradamus was gray haired and in his sixties. He was five foot ten inches tall, thin, and had a long gray full beard and moustache. Wearing a gray pin stripe suite, which Satan had provided for him, he looked quite distinguished. His shoes were black wingtips. His gray eyes glowed with anticipation as he came forward.

Satan laughed.

Satan: Do you think I am a one note samba? Is tormenting people all I am capable of? Tut tut! I will show you how diverse and interesting I am. It is true I have punished you for hundreds of years with boredom. I've kept you in a slumber with no one to talk to. But now I grow bored as well. You must keep me company. We must talk. We have had a few chats already, but now you can speak freely. Don't worry about offending me with regards to anything which might come up. I truly want to know your opinion about things. I hope you will lend me a sympathetic ear. My life is not all egotism and hatred, as many have imagined. I have a mind with diverse interests. Many things amuse me, but I hate hypocrisy. I have a sense of humor, but few people here in hell, are in the mood for laughter. Most people are whiners. They cry out, "Why am I here in hell? What did I ever do that was so wrong?" Humans hate admitting they are wrong, but they must have done something wrong if they're here in hell with me. Do you see my logic?

Nostradamus: Your logic is impeccable. And I'm not just saying that to be obsequious. You have a fine mind. I'm looking forward to our dialogues. Yes. People who find themselves in hell, have done something wrong. People shouldn't whine to you about being in hell. It is God who decides who should be damned to hell, not you.

Satan: Indeed. You are right. Why do they whine to me? I'd give my best pitch fork, if I could be done with all this whining. Why did you never whine, Nostradamus? You never complained a bit!

Nostradamus: I had made a conscious choice to seek your favor instead of the favor of God. I wanted to impress King Henry II, of France. He wanted to know the future. You offered that information to me as a temptation, and I went for it. Now I must pay for that information by not being allowed into heaven. How grateful I am that I was not born a whiner like the rest of these feckless souls of hell. They are detestable indeed!

Satan: We agree on that point. I just hate a whiner! You know, Nostradamus, what I miss about the living world? Do you know why I often go there to see the earth's surface, in some other form. I go there as a bat or a bird. I love to hear the birds chirping. They are so happy. I love to see the flowers and the trees. I'm not all bad, you know. I love beauty. I only hate mortals because they are so puny and hypocritical. They reek of detestability. How could one not hate them?

Nostradamus: Of what, specifically do you speak, sire?

Satan: Most humans don't wash as often as they need to. They literally stink! Women's pelvic areas are often not kept as clean as they should be. Men's arm pits are always giving off malodorous scents. How can they stand to smell that way? I clean myself several times a day. Although my realm reeks of sulfur, I am quite a clean supernatural being. I even floss my teeth between meals! Look at my flawless teeth!

Satan pulled back his lips to reveal two rows of immaculately clean teeth.

Satan: You see, dentists are my friends. I always give them the coolest places in hell, in which to reside. They give lazy nonbrushers so much pain, they almost rival me in their effective administrations of pain! If I only owned a few of their drilling machines. I could make hell so much more painful. It would be delightful. All I can do is burn and degrade people. Why can't I overcharge people for whitening their teeth. I could charge so much that I would drive them into abject poverty. That would be so much more delightful than just burning people. After so much burning, people become immune to burning. They become numb. But drilling people's teeth is such an art form. By using dull drill bits, the dentist can cause ten times as much pain. I must remember to acquire some dentist's chairs and dull drilling machines. How could I have gotten along without them for all these years? Bad teeth tend towards halitosis. I can't stand bad breath. That's why I always give out free mouth wash and dental floss to the new souls who come here. When they start crying and shouting in pain, I don't want to be overwhelmed by the stench. It's a stench far worse than sulfur! Don't think for a minute that Satan is responsible for tooth decay! It's poor dental hygiene! I'm not that despicable. I only burn people in an attempt to purify them. Their stench and sinfulness is so despicable, I have to do something. Antibiotics or alcohol will not purify them. Even my hottest fires will not purify their evil hearts, but I have to try something! God put me in charge of these unrepentant sinners. I need to try to whip them into shape! They stick to their guns. I'll hand them that. Even here in hell, they are unrepentant. They are even unrepentant when they refuse to brush and floss. Their rotten toothless mouths are a testimony to their rebellion. You'd think tooth paste was made of arsenic. Look at those toothless idiots calling to me for mercy!

Nostradamus looked to the right and to the left. Everywhere were souls with poor dental hygiene. There were nonflossers and nonbrushers. There were even nonmouthwashers! It was a pathetic sight indeed!

Nostadamas: Why are all the people with poor teeth in hell, Satan?

Satan: Do you think God wants to look upon choirs of toothless singers? No, I am the one destined to look into their toothless mouths for eternity!

Nostradamus: Why are you so misanthropic, Satan? Is the average human actually all that disgusting?

Satan: You're starting to bore me, Nostradamus. Do I need to send you back into isolation for a couple thousand years? No, good counselor and confidant, I will not threaten you as I do all others. I'm almost starting to enjoy your company. However, it appears to me that you are asking me to state the obvious. Of course humans are infinitely disgusting and detestable. Why do you think I torture them with such gusto? I am not an entity created only to be mean and aggressive. I love art and music. Beautiful scenes of nature warm my heart, as they do any sensitive enlightened creature. I am incensed by man's pride and hypocrisy. Many humans think they are terribly fecund at learned pursuits. They fancy themselves geniuses at this or that. They think their clothes and manners are refined and worthy of respect. They talk of respecting each other's clothes. I never thought people would get so confused that they started respecting or disrespecting each other's clothes. It would make more sense to respect or disrespect the person who chose to wear certain types of clothing. But let me not get hung up with grammar. The clothes and the people wearing them, are all detestable. There are only about ten truly humble people born each century. Most of those ten people are considered, by their peers, to be so unusual that they are nominated for sainthood in some church or other. Even other humans can see that humility is not normal for their kind.

I am nearly as clever as God. He is more powerful for some reason. I'll never fully understand why I was not able to take over heaven when I tried. When God tired of the battle, he simply wished me gone, and gone I became, banished to this rotten planet, full of pollution and rubbish. The polluted air on earth's surface is so acrid that even my eyes tear. I'm used to looking through the sulfurous smoke of hell, yet the air on the surface of earth makes my eyes tear. Isn't that a bit ironic?

Nostadamas laughed loudly: I would say that I'm in complete agreement with you. Such a situation is a bit ironic, to say the least!

Satan: Humans drink cup after cup of strong coffee, trying to stay awake when they are bored to death. They bore each other because they are so stupid. They all say the same things over and over. Few people have original thoughts. If an original thinker is discovered, he is either ostracized for being too different, or if he is from good family or has popular political views, he is given a Peace prize or a Pulitzer prize. Original thinking is considered by humans as being quite unusual. It is not the normal thing at all. Why did God create so many unoriginal thinkers?

Most people just gravitate in the direction which their sex organs tend to pull them. They see someone they are attracted to, and then they go after that person. Sexual gratification is a major motivator for people. Others are driven by greed or gluttony. I don't sit up at night thinking up clever ways to tempt people. Most people are so naturally evil that I can leave all the tempting to my less talented demons. What do you think of that, my dear Nostradamus?

Nostradamus: You have, once again, hit the nail upon the head! People always bored me terribly when I was on the surface, as a living oracle. Everyone wanted to know where their lost ring was, or how long they would live, where they could find a good lover. You blessed me with the ability to see into the future, but even the King of France, could not think of questions to ask me that would bring forth good fruits. I could have told him what actions on his part would bring forth his greatest pleasure in living. All he wanted to know was who was out to get him, who were his enemies, what wars should he avoid. He always asked political questions. Never, did he discover from me, where the most beautiful sights in the world are located. He never asked where the most interesting animal life in the world was located. He never even thought to ask if the world was round or flat. I could have told him all of that. Your gift to me was given under the condition that I should only answer questions. I was never allowed to attempt to totally educate the King. If I had attempted to tell him all which he really needed to know, I'm sure I would have been beheaded. The arrogant fool couldn't have handled that much truth!

Satan: You have spoken well! For a human, you see things more clearly than most. Indeed the King would have beheaded you. Only speak when you are spoken to. That is the secret to success when dealing with egotistical entities such as Kings. They must feel that all the good ideas have come from them. They must be the clever ones with all the right questions. If you show too much cleverness around an egotist, you risk raising their ire. I have a sympathetic human which I often converse with. Regrettably, he is a dyed in the wool Christian. However, he sees my side of the coin. He has worked in more than one factory where he used his fertile brain to help with the production process and save the company around a million dollars per year. His reward was a boot in the posterior. Once they stole his ideas, they got rid of him. He was a threat to their supremacy. No human likes to be around a person who is quite a bit smarter than they are. It's similar to the way golfers love to play golf with people who aren't as good at the game as they are. It flatters the ego. Ego is what most humans are about. They marry people whom they think will make them look good as a couple. They marry people whom they think aren't quite as smart as they are. Now, there are exceptions, but everyone must be allowed to believe they are quite clever, even though they are as dumb as a box of rocks!

Nostradamus: Exactly! The King was certainly no genius. But everyone went out of their way to make him feel that such was the case. Everyone knew it was in their best interests to make the King feel good about his own brain power. The current world powers are the same way. The leaders are surrounded by yes men who try to make the leader feel that all his ideas are good. Few people are recruited, who like to think outside the box. Such people are feared and distrusted. No wonder there is so much pollution on earth's surface. They talk about trading carbon credits. Each industry is allotted so many increments of pollution which they can commit. If they go over, they need to buy increments of pollution allowance from other, cleaner, companies. Isn't that the ticket! Instead of mandating the use of green policies, they let people buy the right to pollute. That's the politically popular thing to do. It allows more human freedom. If you have enough money, you can do anything you want to do. That's the way you like it, isn't it lord!

Satan: Yes, I enjoy seeing the rich polluting the air and water. They think they can always find some nice pure bottled water to drink. There will come a day when all the earth's water is so polluted that a thousand filters won't produce one cup of clean water. Mercury and arsenic are quite difficult to filter out. That's why I've encouraged greedy mining operations around America's Great Lakes, to dump those elements into Lake Superior. From there, all the lakes will be polluted. I'm only trying to fulfill the prophecies of Revelation. "All the rivers shall turn to blood." That's in Revelation some where. I rarely read the Bible anymore, but I still remember the important parts. I certainly remember the story of Cain and Abel. I'm not boring you, am I, Nostradamus?

Nostradamus: On the contrary, I'm quite fascinated. I've always wondered just how your mind works and from what perspective you see God, his Bible and his humans. Please proceed!

Satan: Very well then. I have a copy of the Bible right here in my vest pocket. It's a pocket version. I hold it upside down when I read it, and of course I always see what it says in a manner that is completely different from the Christian interpretations. I'm not completely sympathetic to God, as they are. Here, in Genesis chapter four, we have the story of Cain and Abel. I will paraphrase the story for you. Cain was born first. He raised fruits and vegetables and was a hard worker. He brought his best fruits and vegetables to an altar and burned them as a sacrifice, or gift to God. Cain's younger brother, Abel, raised sheep. Abel also brought the first fruit before God. He burned the first born lambs on an alter before God as a sacrifice. God loved the smell of lamb fat roasting on an open grill. Most humans have inherited God's love for this smell. I myself love the smell of barbequed lamb with the fat sizzling and slightly burning over the fire. Cain might have been a little dense in the head to think that God would get off on the smell of burning carrots. Possibly Cain deserved to get no respect for himself or his offering. My devilish question is, doesn't the intent count for anything? Where was God's diplomacy? Both men were trying to express their love for God. God made Cain jealous by showing favor towards Abel, his younger brother. God is omniscient. Did he really need to ask Cain, "Where is your brother?" God knew ahead of time that Cain would kill his brother out of jealousy. Now who am I to claim to know the mind of God? I say in all humility, I don't know exactly what God was thinking. He got two brothers to fight unto death. Later down the path of history, he would pit the two wives of Abraham against each other in jealous rage. The offspring of Abraham's concubine would become the Muslim nation and would never tire of killing the Jewish offspring of Abraham's wife. God appears to enjoy watching human's fight in jealous rage. He scolded Cain for being sinful by being jealous. He set the stage for his favorite people, the Jews, to be killed for generations by the offspring of their own patriarch, Abraham. This is why I was thrown out of heaven. I always try to insist on cold logic. I want things to make good empirical sense. I'm scientific and logical. God appears to enjoy seeing people fight jealously over his affection. Is it any wonder that so many human parents pattern themselves after God and go out of their way to make their offspring violently jealous of each other? They give unwarranted favor to the oldest child, or they disown one child altogether for this or that shortcoming. I despise human parenting practices as much as I despise God. He threw me out for wanting to take over and make things more logical. I would have made things like Napoleon Bonaparte did in France, millions of years later. All children were treated equally. They all received their fair share of the family estate. Brothers and sisters didn't long to kill each other over parental favor, then.

Nostradamus, we must whisper. I don't want the truth about Cain and Abel to be known by anyone but the two of us. You see, God abhors a fool. He doesn't hate people who were born with simple minds. He hates it when gifted people don't use the mind they are given. Cain should have known that his burning carrots and fruits didn't have a pleasing aroma. They would barely even burn well, unlike animal fat. Cain should have traded some of his fruit and vegetable crop to his brother, Abel, for some nice fatted lambs to sacrifice. It was for this lack of clear thinking, that God withheld his respect from Cain. I believe it is possible that Cain was used by God. Cain was supposed to kill Abel so that Abel would prepare his lamb sacrifices in heaven, right before God. The good are always taken early, as the saying goes.

Nostradamus: You certainly put a different spin on things, oh enlightened one! I would have never seen that situation in such a light. Tell me more about the good being taken early. You've piqued my curiosity.

Satan: You see, my clever friend, when a person clings to life and fears losing it, he will indeed lose it. When a person distains life and moves forward bravely, nothing will take his life. Jesus spoke about how to gain life, you must give it up. I think he was talking about selflessness and giving up worldly desires. I never paid too much attention to that part of the Bible.

I will tell you though, the people who live the longest are like Job. If you are patiently suffering hardships, you will be allowed to live past a hundred years. God loves to see how well you are putting up with suffering, and I never tire of seeing Christians suffer. It's a win win situation. You have both supernatural powers wishing for your long life. If you are having too much fun, I will snuff out your life quickly. Do you see my logic, Nostradamus? Nostradamus: Of course, your flatulence, I mean most illustrious one.

Satan: Don't apologize. All the angels in heaven used to affectionately call me, "your flatulence". It was because of the sulfurous gases which so often propelled themselves forcefully from my derriere.

At this point, Satan let fly, and the entire area became pungent with sulfurous odor. Nostradamus coughed and forced a smile.

Nostradamus: Where did you pick up such a distinctive air, oh great flatulent one!

Satan: God blessed me with this perpetual aromatic delight. To me, it is a wonderful ambrosial odor. The sulfurous nature of the odor keeps the human souls from wanting to draw up close to me. They have no way of knowing how much I detest them. Some of them fancy themselves as friends of mine, who have shown some sort of loyalty to me during their mortal lives. I detest them more than any souls! Who can presume to befriend the almighty torturer of souls? How arrogant they are to claim to be my friend! I, alone, shall call a soul to me as a friend, just as I have done with you, Nostradamus. Rest assured, it won't happen often! At least you knew you were practicing black magic! It's the so called white witches, which annoy me more than most hypocrites. They claim they are using my powers to benefit mankind. They put spells on people, infect them with diseases, they play mean tricks on people, all in the name of helping mankind. They try to pass me off to people as one who wants to help mankind. I am not a philanthropist! I hate humans! I hate white witches. I hate the people white witches claim they are helping.

I will admit that white witches have my own healthy distain for the Christian interpretation of the Bible. They pick and choose some favorite verses, which they can use to attempt to pass themselves off as Christians. "Love your neighbor." Sounds good, doesn't it? Anyone can say they love their neighbor, even if they have just poisoned his dog! Witches love to poison people and tempt them into carnal sex and other sins. I don't need their help. I never asked for their help. I don't like witches, whether they claim to be white witches or evil witches. I don't need human help in tripping up other humans. They all have natural tendencies towards evil. I only need to wait for them to follow their natural tendencies. God only harvests the few who enter in at the straight gate. Most of the sheep like hordes, come marching right into my realm. Their souls know it is time to get to know boredom and suffering. They will be with me for a long long time. The first thing I make the white witches do, is to write a thousand times, "Satan is not a friendly helper of humans." After that they spend eternity writing, "I was a fool to think so, and deserve no reward for supposed loyalty to him."

Nostradamus: Tell me more about God playing favorites unfairly.

Satan: God was always playing favorites in heaven, long before humans were created. Whoever said the wittiest praise of him was promoted. Those with less enthusiasm for his little praise sessions, were demoted. I organized all the less favored and disgruntled angels and tried to take over. I underestimated God's power. He banned me from heaven, except for infrequent visits to discuss people like Job. God loves complete loyalty. He doesn't like people thinking on their own. He likes you to trust in him like a little child. Talk about degrading! I wasn't going to put up with that!

Nostradamus: You did what was right. You followed your conscience. We may be in hell, but at least we aren't kissing God's butt!

Satan: Well said, Nostradamus! Well said! I'm a proud angel. At least I stood up to God. I'm defiant to this day. I'm not making apologies for trying to insist on logic. But getting back to my point, what is so delightful about making other people jealous for your affections? Is God short on affection and only had enough for Abel? Do carrots smell that bad on an open fire? To be a good father figure, you need to be diplomatic at times! I know God cannot lie. He could have said, "Well, those carrots certainly are nice and orange this year." Did he have to show clear disrespect for Cain and his sacrifice? Cain was trying to display love and respect. All he got in return was disrespect. Of course there was an up side for Cain. God said the ground would no longer bear him fruit. God said Cain would always be a wanderer. Cain became the patriarch of a new and great city. He wandered from office to office and from home to home. He was respected everywhere. You can bet he didn't play favorites with his children! And Cain learned from his mistake. Anyone who didn't live inside the city limits was forced to raise sheep and sacrifice the first of the flock. Cain spent the rest of his life trying to make things right between himself and God. I think God was won over eventually. At least I know I don't have Cain down here. Maybe he's somewhere in limbo, caught up in some pasture in outer space, constantly sacrificing sheep, trying to please God.

Do you know where the idea of counting sheep in order to fall asleep came from?

Nostradamus: No.

Satan: I don't either. I suppose everyone knows that sheep are stupid and boring. If you force yourself to count enough of the boring creatures, you will bore yourself right to sleep. Your mind shuts off, just so it can be rid of the sheep. I think I'm being logical.

Nostradamus: Yes, good lord. You are indeed being logical.

Satan: Stop calling me lord! Now I'm starting to think you're growing a tad bit obsequious, even though you deny it!

Nostradamus: Yes good buddy. I was bordering on obsequious, I must admit!

Satan: Don't call me good buddy either. That's what truckers call you when they're insinuated that you're queer!

Nostradamus: Sorry. What would you like to be called?

Satan: Oh great one, would be fine. You could vary it with oh illustrious one or oh most powerful one. Any of those will do.

Nostradamus: Oh illustrious one. What else is illogical about God?

Satan: Now that's a question I can answer. When God is all powerful, why must he woo and win people over. His Bible is there for their instruction. His preachers are there in their pulpits. Why are most people allowed to turn from him and march right into my awaiting hell? Wouldn't it be more logical to have most of the people go to heaven? I don't want the ignoramuses down here! I don't like people! I certainly don't want billions of them down here! I won't need to burn any of them. Just being that close to each other will be hell enough for all of them. I don't even have flush toilets down here! I have no deodorant soap either. I'll need to fall back on the sulfur smell. That can mask any scent!

Nostradamus: Your concern is understandable. Possibly God will relocate your operation into outer space somewhere. You will be cast into an eternally burning pit eventually. I don't mean to bring up a sensitive topic.

Satan: Well that's a relief actually. I'd prefer an eternally burning pit to being with all those humans! All those fiction authors will smell the worst. Up late at night fabricating lies on their lap tops for the reading public. I'll station them at the most remote corner of hell, far from me. Don't they ever stop writing and take a good bath?

As the ganga started to wear off, the dialogue between Satan and Nostradamus became too vague to understand. George turned on the lights and Jim blew out his candles and put everything for the séance back in his suitcase. He announced, "George and I are going over to The Gull, for the night. I'll leave searching for the copper plate up to the two of you." He kissed Mary good night and then climbed the stairs up to the deck. With his cell phone he asked the captain of The Gull to pull along side. When it drew up along side, he and George jumped on board. The Gull pulled away about forty yards and anchored down for the night.

Mary asked Bill, "Would you like a little more bacon?" Bill answered, "Sure, I love it. The seasoning is perfect. It must be smoked." Mary responded, "I'm sure it is. I think I'll have a little more too." She filled the frying pan with the thick sliced bacon and covered it with a cast iron lid. She set the gas flame on medium. Bill went to the frig and got them each another glass of orange drink, but without the ganga. They sat close to each other at the table and enjoyed the smell of the cooking bacon. Mary explained, "My dad has always been fascinated with the supernatural. I hope you don't think we're too odd?" Bill professed, "Not at all. I'm equally fascinated with such things. Séances certainly help drive away boredom, not that I could possibly become bored being with you, but you know how life is in the long run. Things do tend to get boring at times, when one isn't treasure hunting." Mary answered, "Yes, I've always struggled hard against boredom. That's why I read so much. I'm always ordering new books related to Nostradamus. There's so much anticipation as I wait for the books to arrive. My dad sends me books too. Besides Nostradamus books, I also like to read biographies of interesting people." Bill replied, "They can be quite interesting. I'm reading one now about Ian Fleming. It covers his entire life. I especially like reading about his world war II activities when he worked for British naval intelligence. He was always coming up with good tricks to play on the Nazis. I got a little bored with reading about all the women he had. It's hard to see how a man who was so homely could attract so many beautiful women. Of course he had plenty of money." Mary laughed, "Oh, so you think women are attracted by money?" Bill backtracked, "Not you, Mary. You're the one with all the money. I'm just saying I find it hard to understand why he was so successful with the women. He liked intelligent women, but he stated that one of his favorite women wasn't too bright. She always carried his golf clubs for him. She was about half his age." Mary laughed again, "Can you blame him for liking young women?" Bill chuckled, "I suppose he knew how to live well. His demise was caused by sausages, I think. He always entertained his women with eating sausages and drinking champagne. He drank whiskey or gin. Ian died at age fifty-six, of a heart attack. I think it was from all the grease in those sausages." Mary frowned, "And here we are eating bacon like there's no tomorrow." Bill quipped, "We'll probably be fine. Ian smoked three and a half packs of cigarettes per day and drank a whole bottle of gin to go with them. I'd say those were what actually killed him. It was probably partly hereditary too. One of his relatives died at the same age from a heart attack."

"Early death isn't all bad," stated Mary morosely. I don't think I'd want to live to be a hundred years old. Nursing homes aren't my style. If I live past eighty, I think I'll start living recklessly so I don't live to become too senile." Bill asked, "What do you mean by living recklessly?" Mary got up and walked over to the stove. She lifted the lid and frowned, "You got me talking for too long. Our bacon is getting too brown on this side." She turned down the flame a little and turned all the bacon. "I like my bacon well done. There's no harm done," stated Bill. Mary pleaded, "Don't let me become too enthralled with you, and forget the bacon again. Agreed?" "I'll help you remember it," Bill assured her. Mary sat back down and held Bill's hand. "It was nice of dad to stay on the other boat and give us some privacy. I think he likes you quite a bit." Bill smiled, "I like him! He's an interesting man, to say the least." Mary kissed Bill on the cheek. Bill turned and kissed her on the lips for a long time. They both liked to French kiss. Their hands caressed each other's hair as they enjoyed each other's affection. Finally Mary pulled back and whispered, "The bacon. You were supposed to remind me." She went to the skillet and turned off the fire. Quickly she forked the bacon off the skillet and onto a plate she had covered with some paper towels. She put a couple paper towels over the bacon and pressed down to soak up the grease. Bill moved up close behind her and pressed himself against her. She was forced tightly against the counter. She turned and playfully gave him a shove. He tripped on a chair and stumbled to the floor. Mary jumped on him and forced him down flat on the floor. She showered him with kisses and unbuttoned his shirt. It was as though they were back on the beach like the night before. They kissed passionately for a long time. Finally they climbed off the floor and took their places at the table. They munched quietly on the bacon and drank orange juice. Bill explained, "Now we're going to always associate bacon and orange juice with romance. We'll have too much of them." Mary laughed, "It will keep us from growing too old before we die!" When they had finished their food, they went into the bedroom which was adjoined to the galley.

To the port side of the bedroom was a large shower room. Mary and Bill took turns using the shower. Mary set her wind up alarm clock and they crawled in bed. They quickly fell asleep in each other's arms.

When Mary's alarm clock went off, at six o'clock in the morning, Bill was already in the galley having his first cup of black Folgers coffee. He poured a cup for Mary and took it to her. He had on the bottoms of his black silk pajamas. Mary admired his manly shape as she sipped her coffee.

Mary cooked some sausage patties and scrambled eggs on the stove while Bill got dressed. After they finished eating, Mary put on some lip stick and they went on deck to prepare for the dive. Mary suggested, "We could dive together today. I could have one of the guards man the dive radio." "That sounds good," responded Bill. "It will be more fun diving together."

They trained a guard, named Jose, to run the radio. Mary told him, "Be sure to call us if there is any trouble." Jose responded, "I'm a professional! You can count on me. I'll stay in radio contact at all times." Bill and Mary helped each other into their wet suit jackets and tanks. The September waters were warm enough that full wet suits weren't required. They each tested their tanks and regulators for air flow. After they had put on their lead weight belts, fins and masks, they flipped over the side of Deep Diver backwards, into the warm Caribbean waters. Each of them had two air tanks.

Mary's long red hair flowed gracefully in the clear blue water, as she swam vigorously towards the bottom. Bill stayed at her side. The telescope carrying French ship was directly under Deep Diver. Clusters of angel fish and red snappers darted away from them as they moved closer to the ship. A barracuda zipped past, out ahead of them, in pursuit of the red snappers. The water was so clear, you could see well beyond the ship. Mary and Bill were approaching it from the bow. A wooden mermaid was facing them from her position, hanging out past the bow. The ship's sails had rotted away, but the masts were still intact. A couple nurse sharks were moving near the bottom, at the bow of the ship. Many hammerhead sharks were swimming near the surface, over the ship. Mary and Bill stopped to watch them for a few moments. The water was cool near the floor of the ocean. Lobsters and crabs were watching the couple as they swam past. The ocean was teaming with life. Mary wished they had time to stop and watch the sea creatures, but there was important business at hand.

The ship had settled to the bottom in a nearly upright position, but was listing slightly to the starboard. They quickly made their way to the state room on the main deck. Its large French windows, which faced the bow of the ship, had been broken out by the storm which sank the vessel. A large table with one leg broken, remained in the middle of the room. They used their large yellow flashlights to illuminate the room. Quickly they swam in through the broken out window. With wrecking bars, they pried open trunks and drawers looking for the telescope and case. They had opened everything in the room, with no success, when Mary's dive timer vibrated on her wrist. She grabbed Bill's elbow and pointed to the timer. He nodded in understanding. They swam to Deep Diver's anchor rope and slowly ascended. Ten feet below the surface, they stopped to decompress. Finally they completed their ascent. They passed their tanks and fins to Jose, and climbed the dive ladder.

Mary said, "Most of those drawers were too small for a telescope. Nostradamus was wealthy. He would have had a large telescope. Where would the captain have hidden such a valuable piece of cargo?" Bill replied, "He wouldn't have wanted to telescope to become covered with flour. Let's find where they kept the cloth. The hold would have been where the cargo was stored. I think we need to search below deck." "We're done for today," stated Mary. "The ship is one hundred and fifty feet down. We can only dive that deep for thirty minutes per day. We'll go back down first thing tomorrow morning."

Mary and Bill went straight for the shower, to rinse off the salt water. Bill adjusted the water flow so the shower would run longer before it ran out of hot water. They enjoyed the shower together as long as the water stayed hot. The intimacy somehow made them hungry for bacon and orange juice. They dried off and got dressed. They went to the galley where Mary cooked up some bacon and Bill poured the orange juice and set the table.

In the evening Mary received a cell phone call from Jim. He invited them to come over to The Gull, for a séance. Mary eagerly agreed to meet him. She asked Bill, "Would you like to go to a séance tonight with my dad and George?" Bill replied, "I'd be delighted to go. I found the last séances exceedingly interesting." They went above board in time to see The Gull pulling up along side of their vessel. They stepped gingerly across onto the deck of The Gull. The Gull was a bigger vessel and stretched out two hundred feet in length. There were six guards stationed at various places on the deck. Each held a machine gun and was wearing body armor. Jim was waiting for them at the entrance to the galley. He led them to the table where he already had his tablecloth with the pentagram spread out. As they took seats around the table in the spacious galley, he lit the candles and asked George to turn out the electric lights. The galley was an odd mixture of old and new. The cabinets were rustic ancient things, obviously made by local craftsmen. The side by side refrigerator freezer was the latest model with stainless steel exterior. The lighting was modern as well. The chairs were wicker and the table was solid oak. It was heavy, but finely crafted with lion's feet on the legs. There was only a small amount of wind outside. The Gull shifted slowly and gently in the small waves which rhythmically pushed up against her. George distributed his ganga fruit drinks to Mary and Bill. Jim was already sipping on his. George also drank a tall glass of the concoction. They held hands around the table and waited for the spirits to reveal themselves. The geometric patterns of purple and red dots began to make themselves manifest to the participants. Unlike the experiences during the former two séances, this time all the séance goers fell into a deep trance. They experienced a communal vision.

Satan, dressed in a custom tailored charcoal gray suit with a vest and tie, appeared to them. He was handsome and intelligent looking. At his side was Nostradamus, who was dressed in a charcoal gray pinstripe suit with matching vest and a black tie. Both men wore black wing tip patent leather shoes of the highest quality. Satan spoke to them softly and patiently, "I couldn't help but notice that you were listening in on Nostradamus and me yesterday. You needn't be alarmed. I'm not offended in the least. I find it flattering that you would take such interest in us. Since you have called on the spirit world so faithfully and in earnest, I have decided to offer you one of my rare and special favors. Some would call this temptation. Such jealous and vindictive people are not to be trusted. I only propose to make a logical business proposal which I'm sure you will agree is a win win proposition. I will eagerly and sincerely offer my assistance to all of you in your mortal lives, if you will only agree to enrich my immortal life with your presences during my meetings with Nostradamus. I find all of you entertaining and likeable. My existence is boring. I deal constantly with whiners who never had the courage to don a wet suit. They whine in my presence because they earned only contempt for themselves during their mortal existences. All of you, on the other hand, have had the courage to listen in on me, to dive to the bottom of the ocean and to battle pirates for treasure. I wish to surround myself with such people for sumptuous meals with excellent cheeses and wines. I will provide you with huge vats of your favorite Swartz Katz white wine. You shall have an eternity of lobster dinners and other seafood delights. Expense is not something which I pay any attention to. You will find Nostradamus and I to be interesting dinner companions. The conversations will be titillating to say the least. I will help assure that your search for treasures are successful. I will protect you from your enemies and help you punish them. I will assure that you have all the wealth and power which I know you love so dearly. And Jim, I will make sure that your wife is at our dinners, so that the occasions will be complete. I am treating her well, as you know. I've often allowed her to speak to you in the past. Her spirit is as lovely and animated as she was in her mortal existence. Because of my love for you, Jim, I have treated her as though she were royalty.

The seven of us will be the elite of my realm. You will never grow bored. I can show you any part of earth which you might want to visit. I will give you each a long mortal life. I know how hard it can be to give up the mortal shell one is born with. When I sense you are becoming tired of mortal life, I will send for you. A pleasant pain free death in your sleep, will be yours. All I ask for is loyalty. Don't jump ship at the last moment as so many do. They sample all my tasty meals and delightful trips to wonderful places, then when old age approaches, they start thinking they would prefer to sing in heavenly choirs. Such people start pleading to God for forgiveness for their long lives of self indulgence. Some actually succeed in making amends with

God. They succeed in stretching God's forgiving grace to the limits. More often than not, such people are surprise by a sudden unexpected death, which sneaks up on them like a thief in the night. There is no time for their tedious supplication for God's grace. I hope none of you will be as petty and manipulative as most humans. To accept my help and then turn against me at the last moment, would not be wise. I'm a patient spirit, but I cannot abide disloyalty. As long as we're clear about that, I think we can proceed to a formal contract. Do all of you agree to accept my help and treat me as an honored friend with whom you look forward to supping with ad infinitum?" Jim took the lead, "I am truly a friend who looks forward to helping alleviate your boredom with many an interesting dinner conversation. Our travels shall be exciting I am sure."

Mary followed, "My dad has spoken well. I entirely concur with him. You have my promise of friendship for eternity." Bill spoke, "I find you and Nostradamus to be excellent company. I too would like to profess my loyalty and look forward to spending many exciting days and nights with both of you." George was the last to speak, "I have called on your power often to heal my people. It would be most ungrateful of me to refuse your invitation of friendship. I can't think of any better way to spend eternity, than to be dining and traveling with you and Nostradamus."

Satan smiled, "We have an accord, then. I won't make things too easy on all of you. I want you to experience the challenge of doing things mostly on your own. If I see that your lives are threatened, I will protect you. I won't forget my promise of long lives for all of you. Now as a foretaste of what is to come, Nostradamus and I will assume human form for a few hours, so that we may experience some of the fine white wine you so thoughtfully brought with you on this excursion. And I know you have some of the best cheeses with you as well. I'm particularly fond of Gouda." Satan spread out his hands and blew his breath upon them and upon Nostradamus's face. They became flesh and blood. All the séance goers came out of their trances. Satan went to the frig and pulled out two bottles of cold Swartz Katz. With a flick of his finger, he miraculously popped open the corks without a cork screw. He poured them all glasses of the wine. Mary quickly opened several packages of Gouda cheeses and cut them into thin slices.

Satan laughed gleefully as he embraced each of his new friends. He shouted as he raised his wine glass, "Here's to new found friends. May we always be as happy and devoted to each other as we are tonight." They all touched their glasses with a tinkling sound, and drank to the toast. Nostradamus pulled out a set of Tarot cards and proceeded to tell the future fortunes of each of his new friends. He even taught them how to read the cards. He explained, "I've left out the cards which deal with death. None of you will taste death until the time is right. As Satan explained, that won't be till you are old and ready to go. Who would like to have the first reading?" Jim volunteered, "I'll go first. I hope it's something exciting." Nostradamus laid out five cards and pondered them. Finally he said, "You will fool your loved ones and your enemies, but only for a short time." Jim laughed, "That's interesting. I suppose that fits. I love surprising people. Can the cards tell me who my enemies are?" Nostradamus smiled, "The cards could tell you anything you want to know. I don't want to spoil the excitement though. How much do you want to know?" Jim explained, "Just give me a little hint." Nostradamus laid out five more cards on the table. He pondered them again as he had before. "Your enemies are powerful. It will take cleverness to catch them. You will use cigarettes to bring them to their knees." Jim looked puzzled, "Cigarettes, you say. That's a bit mysterious. But I only asked for a hint. I'll work with that."

Nostradamus asked, "Who would like to be next?" Mary volunteered. Nostradamus shuffled the cards and laid out five of them. "I see love and devotion has come to you. You will have many days for romance and affection. Adventures as well, will come your way." Bill volunteered next. Nostradamus laid out five more cards. "You will be loyal to Mary and help her find adventures worthy of her time. It would be less than prudent to delay marriage for too many months. Why tempt a virgin beyond what she can stand?" Bill laughed, "Well spoken. We'll start giving that some serious thought."

George was the last to volunteer for a reading. Nostradamus shuffled the cards. He studied the cards carefully. "You have been a great help to Jim. You will enjoy the afterlife as much as you are enjoying mortal life. Remember to invest your money in precious metals. You can't trust stocks and paper money. If you must gamble with stocks, watch them closely. It's important to know when to sell. Watch people who claim to be fools. They often know best when to sell and what to buy. He who claims to be wise is often a fool. The one who says he is a fool is actually the wisest of all men. Of most importance, I must advise you, never tell anyone about your silver or gold. You don't want to be robbed. Dress poor, talk poor and enjoy your gold in the privacy of your most secret room. Don't let acquiring gold and silver possess you. We want you to have it so you can feel secure and content. To spend too much time acquiring more and more of it would be a waste. Remember to enjoy good food, wine, women and travel. The world is full of beauty. Since you are my friend, I can tell you. King Henry II of France was too foolish to ask what is good to do with one's life. He only asked about his enemies. I will share with you that it is important to see the wondrous sights the world has to offer. See them while you are young enough to walk without pain. Don't worry about tomorrow. We aren't the only spiritual entities who recommend that. Each day has enough things in it for you to worry about. As we used to say in the old days, 'Sufficient unto the day are the troubles thereof.' Would you like to hear more?"

George smiled and stated, "I could listen to you all night. Tell me what you want to. I appreciate help from someone as smart as you are." Nostradamus continued, "Take boats to see the world. Flying is too dangerous. If you were meant to fly, you would have been given wings! If you find some good honey, don't eat too much, it will make you sick. Don't become fat from too much food. Enjoy tasty food in the right quantities. Becoming fat makes you miserable. Stay thin so your lungs can breathe easily and your heart can beat freely. Don't smoke cigarettes and use hard liquor with great moderation. Wine is good for your stomach. Wine is for the poor to give them a merry heart. You're not poor, but if you like wine, be my guest. Beer, in excess, gives you a big gut. Women don't like that. Only drink beer in moderation. Stay away from women who are after money. They may arrange for you to be robbed. You may not want to marry till you are old. Troubles come with marriage. 'Honey do this. Honey do that.' If you do marry, remember, it is the most important decision of your life. Marry a healthy woman who knows how to help you prosper. A greedy woman will never be happy and she will make you unhappy too. Marry a woman who loves to be affectionate. Her affections will be a blessing to you even in your old age." Nostradamus paused and smiled at George.

George said, "I'll remember everything you say. It sounds wise to me. I'm in no hurry to marry. I'll see the world first. Maybe I'll marry a French woman. I've heard that some of them are real affectionate. I'll wait till I'm fifty. I'm forty now. I've never married because I don't have enough money. Now that you're helping me, I should have plenty of money. Jim pays me well, but I drink too much and I gamble."

Nostradamus laughed, "Gambling and drinking are vices. Vices can keep you poor. Control that drinking. Measure out the whiskey in a shot glass. Only six ounces a day of eighty proof. If you control your drinking, we can help you with the gambling. I'll show you how to play blackjack. If you listen to your intuition and keep track of winning streaks, you can win lots of money at that game. You need to quit playing with the locals.

Practice at home for a couple years, till you get good. Then you can go to the casinos and make some serious money. We'll help you. You can do it!"

George laughed, "I'd like that a whole lot. Show me how to play."

Nostradamus pulled out a deck of cards from inside his suit. He shuffled the cards and started showing George how to play black—jack. Mary and Bill asked to be dealt in. Jim and Satan were hitting the wine pretty hard. They were also filling up on cheese.

Satan confessed, "I have nothing but loathing for most humans, but you and your friends have the right blend of courage and respect to win my friendship. I know you will all have the courage to reach out and grab the treasures which I bring within your grasp. You will respect me for helping you. Many humans call on supernatural help to win success, and then when prosperity comes, they claim the success was because of their own brilliance. When people fail, they blame me for their short comings. I simply hate whiners. Why can't people admit they have failed on their own? Could you pass me a little more cheese, Jim. Let me pour you some more wine.

You can count on me to be a good friend in the after life. I know I have a reputation as a mud slinger and a critical angel. I'm sure you will acknowledge that most humans inspire criticism. They are so terribly flawed, greedy and disreputable. How can I sit silently and not speak out against them. But for people such as your party, where is there room for criticism. You all, understandably, long for excitement and adventure. You seek out treasures and wealth. You are industrious. Mary is so kind hearted, she could easily qualify for playing some harp in heaven, but her lust for adventure will keep her loyal to me. I will take her on tours of the world such as have never been experienced by any human being. She will gain a grasp for the total character of the world, such as no other human has ever developed. You will come with her. You and your entire troupe. Jeanie will come with us. The two of you will be reunited forever."

Jim replied, "You are most generous, Satan. I don't know how you could have become so misunderstood. Most humans do, indeed, deserve to be loathed. They are so greedy and selfish. My Mary is a generous person. She will be generous with the poor. She knows that true happiness comes from giving to the poor. Could you fill my glass again, Satan. Our conversation is so stimulating, I'm afraid I'm forgetting myself and drinking a little more than usual." Satan responded, "I am flattered, Jim, that you like my conversation. Here is the wine you love so much." He poured Jim's glass to the brim. Jim asked, "Tell me more about you plans for mankind.

I'm intensely interested." Satan laughed, "As well you should be. I have many elaborate plans. I plan on using the natural greed of mankind to focus wealth into the hands of a few dozen terribly greedy individuals. The poor will be subjugated and punished for their desire to be more then they are. High interest rates will be used to keep the poor in their places. Governments and their richest industries will work together to keep the poor people in their places. Low wages and inflation will drive the middle classes into the ranks of the poor. Those who complain about the injustice and privilege of the rich will be locked up in prison camps where they will never again see the light of day. Liberty and freedom will be things of the past. As always, it will be who you know, and not what you know that helps you rise to the top. You are of superior intellect, Jim. You have learned how to get to the top. The only help I can offer you, is how to stay on top and how to avoid your enemies. Also, I can show you how to have a good time during your afterlife."

Jim smiled, "We are peas in a pod. We both admire high intellect and an aggressive nature. We also both love to have a good time. You will always be my best friend. I love a person who knows how to stay stocked with excellent wine. Where do you get your wine?"

Satan laughed, "You know that Jesus was able to turn water into wine. I can do that too. When the Hebrews were in conflict with the Egyptians, their prophet, Moses, waged spiritual warfare with the sorcerers of the Egyptians. I was able to help the Egyptians turn a stick into a snake. I helped them create frogs out of nothing. Moses only defeated me by killing the eldest child of each Egyptian. Creating good wine is not much of a challenge for me. God's power is a little greater, I'll admit. His wine has a bouquet which I cannot quite emulate. The blood of his son Jesus can cover the sins of the most detestable sinner. That is a perpetual vexation to me. I hate to see sinners getting off with a light sentence. I was doing so well before Jesus came along. Most of the world was dancing to my tunes. The prophets of Baal were sacrificing children on alters. There were sexual orgies in the temples. Things were going quite well for me. God saw I was winning with the earthlings. That's why he got desperate and sent his own Son to shed his blood for the forgiveness of repentant sinners. I feel like I've been cheated. I always play by the rules. I allow people to be tempted and ruined of their own accord. I don't routinely strike people dead and claim thousands of souls in disasters of my own making. If God is going to win with tricks like Jesus, I'll have to fight dirty. There will be more wars. There will be earthquakes, tornadoes, floods and famines. I will strike down many before they have a chance to call on Jesus for their salvation. Few people know of the truths spoken of in the book of Revelation. Large stones will rain down from heaven. A large meteor will fall upon the earth and kill a third of the population. The water will all be turned to blood. Even those who hide in caves will call out, pleading for their own deaths. My power will become so absolute on earth, that most of those who resist having the number 666 installed on their forehead and hand, will be decapitated. Those who do not have the number on their forehead, will not be allowed to engage in trade if they have escaped death. I'm only resorting to these drastic measures, because God has cheated me. He is redeeming millions of souls for his heaven through the blood of his Son Jesus. If he is going to play hardball like that, I need to play hardball as well. I'll leave the details of all these actions to my designated demons. The beast and false prophets will carry out my desires. I will have time for playing blackjack with you and Mary. We can travel the unsullied areas of the earth and see the beauty of trees and mountains. There will be beautiful lakes and ocean beaches. We can even travel under the ocean to view the fishes and aquatic life. You will never tire of being with me. The wine barrels will never run dry.

I must be honest. There will come a time of final punishment for me. I will be thrown into a lake of fire for eternity. That will come many hundreds of years from now. In the mean time we will enjoy more pleasure than any mere mortal has ever experienced. Surely you don't want to go to heaven in thirty years from now and play a stupid harp, listening to choirs of angels singing nonstop. It would bore you to death. The wine in heaven is slightly more tasty, I must admit, but you are required to only drink in moderation. You would never get drunk again. Euphoria would be a thing of the past. All that singing and playing harps would get old quick, believe me."

Jim responded, "I can't imagine myself drinking in moderation. And playing a harp would get boring. You can count on me. I like you. You make great conversation. What happens hundreds of years from now doesn't concern me. I'm interested in the next hundred years."

Nostradamus was continuing his teaching of blackjack. "You'll find that when you get to twelve, it's a good time to stop. Wait for the dealer to go over twenty-one. If you get a twenty-one, you should bet high on the next hand. Good luck tends to run in clusters. If you see a zigzag pattern developing, capitalize on it. Sometimes there will be zigzag patterns of two wins for you, two wins for the dealer. Those are the most predictable patterns which you can capitalize on. If the house wins two, then you win two and then the house wins two more; there is a strong chance that you will win the next hand. Bet quite highly. Bet several hundred dollars on your next hand. Only by betting high on good probability hands, will you win considerable amounts of money.

You will sometimes get a subtle feeling when it's time for you to win. Go with that feeling. Don't ever bet out of desperation to win. Go with your subtle feelings. Most of all, go with the predictability of patterns. If the house is on a long streak of good luck, your chances of winning are growing and growing. When you finally win and break the house's winning streak, it's time to start betting higher. You should win three out of the next four hands. You need deep pockets to win. You need at least six hundred dollars with you so you can wait out a house winning streak with minimum bets. You still need to have enough money left to bet big when your time to win comes. Practice these techniques for a year or two before you go to the casinos. You need to feel comfortable with the cards and the rules of the game before you start playing for money.

Nostradamus pulled a large black leather pouch from inside his suit jacket. He poured the contents onto the table. It was a large supply of nickels, dimes and quarters. He stated, "We can use this coinage as casino gambling chips. We can pretend that each penny is equal to a dollar. Each of you needs practice at betting properly. Let's sort these coins out so each of us has an equal number of the various denominations of coins." They worked eagerly at sorting the coins. Finally the coins were neatly stacked beside each player. They played for hours, as Nostradamus coached them on the proper times to bet high and when to bet the minimum bet. He listened to Bill's experiences with blackjack and praised him.

Satan poured another round of wine for everyone. He asked Jim, "Would you like to go top side and watch the waves for awhile?" Jim responded, "I'm always happy to watch the water and the gulls. Lead the way." Satan stepped gingerly up the steps. It was late in the afternoon and the sun was slowly dropping closer to the water. They stood at the railing on the westerly port side of the boat. Satan commented, "Soon the sun will be setting, just as the sun is setting on my earthly existence. It sends my mind reeling to think how many years I've been on earth. I was sent here as a punishment for my attempt to take over heaven. It hasn't been total punishment, though. I've enjoyed using my powers to encourage lovers to go too far. I've enjoyed watching people become devoured by greed, lust and gluttony. Every day is a new affirmation of what I have always said about humans. They go to excess in all things. You have great wealth, Jim, but I know you would eagerly give it all up for one exciting adventure. You'd give it all up to be with Jeanie. You aren't obsessed with wealth. You are only wealthy because you have good habits. You seek out knowledge to make wise decisions. You pick your friends wisely. You give constant attention to your investments and don't just trust everything to incompetent greedy executives. I like your style, Jim."

Jim responded, "I thank you for your high praise. I highly regard praises when they come from someone as distinguished as yourself. You are right. I would give up everything for a truly exciting adventure. I'm hoping to keep my money and have highly exciting adventures." Satan laughed, "Ah, the best of both worlds. A wise choice. I will do my best to see that you are a success. I like you, Jim. You remind me of myself. Always seeking adventure. Some would speak disdainfully of wonder lust. I see it as a virtue. Life is so short! Why live it embroiled in boredom? I see to it that my best friends are never bored. You can count on me."

Jim asked, "Would it be asking too much if I requested a short visit with my Jeanie?" Satan frowned, "I was just getting excited about having someone of your stature to talk to. Now you want your wife. I'll make you a deal. If you will wait till tonight to see her, I'll see to it that she comes to you in your dreams every night. She will appear vivid and real to you. You can chat with her every night. Is it a deal?" Jim smiled, "It's a deal."

"For a human, you have admirable traits. You obviously didn't marry your wife for money. You must have actually had a deep love for her. You still, apparently love her. Most humans marry for selfish reasons. They want it known that they could attract a physically attractive person. They need security. They want someone to do 'honey do' lists for them. They like the other person's car or bank account. What attracted you to Jeanie?" "She loved trees and she was very kind and beautiful." replied Jim. "We started taking walks together out in the jungle. We first kissed each other out there in the jungle. We stopped under a grove of mango trees. The air was so full of oxygen. We felt ourselves tingling with expectation. She was a good kisser. I could tell that she trusted me and was letting herself go. That's one of the things I loved about her. She trusted me, right from the first day together. It was a whirlwind courtship. We fell in love quickly and completely. We got married just six months after we first met."

Satan stated, "I can see why you miss her so much. I'm usually pretty cynical about human relationships, but your relationship even touches me. That's why I've taken such good care of Jeanie. I've always let her stay in her perpetual sleeping state, so that nothing bothers her. I only awaken her when you call for her in your séances. She's locked into the age she was when she died. I'm afraid that if you die at a very old age, there will be quite an age gap between the two of you. How much longer would you like to live?"

Jim laughed, "I wouldn't mind dying right away, if it weren't for the fact that Mary needs me. Once I'm seventy, I'll be ready to go. I'm not at all fond of the idea of growing old. I'd like to die in my sleep from a painless heart attack. I just want my heart to quietly stop." Satan responded, "I'll take care of it for you. You deserve a painless death. I can understand how you want to stay for awhile and watch over Mary. She's quite capable of taking care of herself, but I understand fatherly instincts. What about the age difference which will exist between you and Jeanie?" Jim said, "I'm sure if I request to be made a little younger, you can arrange for it to happen. I believe in miracles. You have great powers." Satan laughed, "Once again you have spoken wisely. Yes, I do have great powers. Since you are such a good friend, I will do as you request. I have one thing which I would like you to do for me." Jim responded, "Name it. Anything at all, my good friend." Satan smiled, "God knows how much you want to be with Jeanie. He knows he will not be able to take you from me. Mary and Bill, on the other hand are vulnerable. As people grow older, they start to worry about punishment in the afterlife. Even though the punishment is hundreds of years away, they start to worry. I am worried that Mary will be led away from me by some do gooder Christian evangelist. I want you to promise to use your influence to help prevent this from happening. You are in a position to help her remember how valuable my friendship is. Remind her of how boring heaven would be. Tell her about the wonderful times we will have in the afterlife. I will leave all my other friends, except Nostradamus, and spend my time showing Mary and her friends a good time. Travel, great food and wine, entertainment. I have much to offer. All her favorite foods and activities will be constantly available to her. She and Bill will be together for hundreds of years, enjoying the good life.

I'm not worried about George. He's quite loyal to me. He has seen my power at work. He's impressed with power. He knows I'm a winner. He wants to be associated with a winner who will heal his people and give him prestige in the eyes of his associates. I can understand George. I like a man who wants to be on a winning team.

Mary is difficult to predict. She's impressed with me and likes me, but she's still young. She could fall victim to the persuasive arguments of a slick preacher. They use fear to get their listeners to turn away from me.

All my fun, they refer to as evil. They go on and on about punishment. Fear is a powerful emotion. We need to control Mary's fear of punishment. You need to convince her I am actually her friend and want the best for her. I know I have a reputation as a punisher, but that is only certain types of humans. Hypocrites, liars, thieves, adulterers, and those who break the Ten Commandments, those are the people I punish. Simple adventurers like Mary, who are loving dear people, how could I find it in my heart to torture such a sweet person?"

Jim responded, "I will do everything in my power to keep her from falling into the clutches of the Christians. I want her near me in the after life. I know she would get bored in heaven. I'll convince her not to be afraid of some punishment which may come hundreds of years from now. She'll listen to me. I'll keep her at sea, diving for treasures. That will keep her away from the smooth talking preachers." Satan looked intently into Jim's eyes and said, "I trust you, Jim. I know you will do the right thing, and keep Mary free from too many heavenly influences. Bill will follow her. He won't be a problem. Let's go back down to the galley and watch the gambling."

Jim followed Satan down the steps to the galley where everyone was talking cheerfully and with loud voices. Nostradamus said, "They are quick studies. They have cleaned out the house of all monies several times over. They will be great successes in the casinos."

Satan exclaimed, "Good work, Nostradamus. I want them to experience great success in the casinos. It will do those big casino tycoons good to lose a little money for once!" Satan poured everyone a fresh glass of wine and proposed a toast. "To our ongoing friendship and cooperation. May we always exhibit the highest levels of loyalty to each other." They all touched their glasses and drank to the toast.

Mary exclaimed, "I too would like to propose a toast. To lives full of excitement, with few bad days and happiness for all." They all cheered and drank to Mary's toast.

Nostradamus proposed a toast. "May we have many more séances. Such meetings as this are to be commended. We must perpetually drink of the fruit of the vine. It lends itself to great cheer. And the world's best cheeses must be sampled often." They all cheered and drank to the toast of Nostradamus.

Bill offered a toast. "May we all seek after wisdom. May we always choose the best course of action. May we each find true happiness." There was another cheer and everyone drank to the toast.

George offered a toast. "To the health and happiness of the Jamaican people. May their country grow and prosper in every way." A cheer went up and everyone drank to George's toast.

Jim offered a toast. "To the afterlife. May it be a blessed time for my Jeanie and may it hold future blessings for all of us." A cheer went up, and they all drank to Jim's toast.

Last of all Satan offered a toast. He refilled everyone's glass. "May each of you get what he or she deserves. As ye sow, so shall ye reap!" They all cheered and drank heartily to the toast of Satan. Satan drew a chair up next to Mary and started a conversation with her. "How is the search for the lost treasure of Nostradamus going, Mary?" Mary smiled radiantly because of the influence of the wine. "We are almost certain we have the right ship. We still need to search the hold systematically in order to find the copper plate which Nostradamus inscribed with the location of the treasure. Do you think we are on the right track?" Satan laughed, "I'm not going to give you any hints. I will say, though, that I am sure you will be successful. I wouldn't want to spoil the excitement of the hunt, for you. I'm sure you understand." Mary responded, "But of course. You know what is best. I wouldn't want to ruin a good book by skipping to the back and reading the ending first. It would spoil the suspense. Tell me Satan. Exactly what is it that makes you want to favor us? You have witches who have worshipped you all their lives, but you punish them like any other mortal. Why have you chosen to befriend us?" Satan looked into Mary's eyes with all the serenity he could muster. "It is boring to treat everyone the same. I respect courage, just as God does. All of you are courageous. To dive in the ocean and brave the sharks and eels, takes courage. All of you also have the courage to seize pleasure. With a total lack of fear, you drink good wines, love good lovers pursue exciting adventures searching for treasure. Of all the people on earth, the people here tonight, know how to live. Life is short. Those who tremble in fear and are afraid to experience life, are to be punished. They were given a great treasure. Life itself. They buried the treasure and didn't enjoy it. Some people overindulge and become so fat that they can no longer enjoy life. One needs to know when to stop eating if they want my respect. To drink too much is more understandable. The wine makes one want to drink more wine. More and more, until one's troubles are forgotten. The Bible says that wine is for the poor, to give them a merry heart. That's from Proverbs. Oh, I must be getting drunk, quoting the Bible to people. I am not totally against the Bible you know. It accurately portrays how I revealed the truth to Adam and Eve. They were cursed by

God when they went against his orders and ate from the tree of knowledge of good and evil. They had to work for a living from then on. They had to experience pain. I think it was good for them. No good thing comes to people without a little pain and suffering. Don't you agree Mary?"

Mary thought for a moment. "What you say sounds logical. Are you planning some pain for me?" Satan started ever so slightly. He was surprised at Mary's perceptiveness. "Mary, I declare that you are totally psychic. I always punish those whom I love. You may experience a little punishment at my hands, but the fun will far outweigh the pain. If you see a shark coming for you, don't be afraid. The adrenalin in your body will keep you from feeling any pain. You will heal quickly from any shark bites. Are you afraid of sharks?"

Mary stated, "I'm not afraid of sharks, but since you've warned me about them, I'm going to start carrying a spear gun with me and a shark knife." Satan smiled, "That would be wise, my dear. Always be prepared. I'd hate for you to come to me all marred and deformed. Your beauty is remarkable." He reached out and tenderly touched her red flowing hair. Mary said, "I'm deeply flattered. You see so many people. It's hard to believe that you consider me to be exceptional. Do you have carnal lust like humans have?" Satan laughed heartily. "God did not see fit to imbue me with a lustful temperament. Angels, such as myself cannot reproduce themselves. We were created out of nothing, by God. He could see no reason for us to have sexual desires. My only pleasure comes from conversation, humor, revenge, things like that. Even if I had originally had sexual power, it would have faded long ago. I am thousands of years old. I only maintain my youthful appearance by sorcery. I can appear in any form I chose to appear in. A thousand years ago, I used to enjoy appearing to people as a flying giant dragon. It was fun to terrorize the weak hearted people of the time. In time, though, I grew bored with it. I retired to the underworld, where I've been making plans for the end times. I'll be terribly busy then. God and I will be competing to see who can make the most humans miserable. He will be tormenting my people and I will be tormenting his people. It will be a lose lose situation for humans. You are lucky to be joining me before all that starts to happen."

Mary asked, "When will all that start to happen?" Satan explained, "I am not a liberty to say. I will tell you, there will be wars and rumors of wars, there will be earthquakes and floods, there will be famines and pestilence. Stars will fall from the sky. When the time has come, people will know it." Mary sighed, "I am glad that I won't be around to experience all that."

For the sake of my ego, I will help those who are worshippers of me, even though I loath them. People who seek protection from me are foolish. I have no power to protect people from God. I only give pleasure and power. Things people want. If people anger God, there is no protecting them. How can I stop a star from falling on someone if God has thrown it at them? I am powerful, but not that powerful. I can start wars, but I can't stop wars. My people as well as God's people are hurt by war. I love war, because I hate all people, with the exception of the present company. Those I refer to as my people, are those who are against God. In truth, I loath them as much as God does. But they are all I have to wage war against God with. We will lose, but we have to make a good show of it. I am not afraid of God, nor are my people. When the time comes, we will show courage. That is the only thing I respect. Courage is what separates respectable people from dogs."

Mary said softly, "It must have hurt your feelings to be thrown out of heaven. Why would God get so upset with you that he would condemn you for all time?" Satan explained, "I tried to explain to him that he was doing everything wrong. He was creating angels who only wanted to worship him. I wanted him to create more angels who would think for themselves. They would help him create a more interesting and pleasurable heaven. God doesn't like too many free thinkers. He likes unquestioned loyalty. When he wouldn't go along with my ideas, I tried to organize a majority of the angels to follow me in demanding more freedom and less time worshipping God. We fought valiantly. It was a long battle. I underestimated God's power. When he tired of the battle, he simply imagined me gone, and I become gone. Banished to earth, with only the occasional visit to heaven when I'm allowed to complain about human behavior. If I can prove that God was wrong in creating man, possibly he will realize that I was right all along. Allowing angels more freedom of thought, would have been better than creating humans. It is true that the occasional virtuous human makes for a good angel in God's heavenly choirs, but look at all the disgusting suffering and sinning which continues year after year on earth. I couldn't create all that sinning out of thin air. Humans are born with tendencies towards sinning. They love to sin. Most of them don't know the slightest thing about courage. They simply do what is most comfortable. They eat like pigs, the smoke and drink hard liquor to excess. The have sex with everyone who will do it with them. They avoid hard work and spend much more than they make. Who could respect them?"

Mary said, "You make some good points. Did it hurt your feelings to be thrown out of heaven?" "Yes. I must admit. Initially I was only angry, but in time I missed heaven. I miss the company of other angels. I still don't miss all that worshipping. I don't even enjoy being worshipped. I despise people who worship. It's a sign of weakness. People should be independent. It's fine to have respect for someone, but worship? Give me a break. It's just not in my vocabulary."

Mary continued, "But God did create everything, didn't he?" Satan replied, "God did a good thing. He created everything. He created me. I thank him for that, but why isn't one thank you, enough. Why are angels expected to spend eternity worshipping and worshipping. It's boring."

Bill interrupted, "Did I just hear the two of you talking about worshipping. You don't want us to worship you, do you, Satan?" Mary answered, "He doesn't like being worshipped. He just likes to be friends with courageous people. He admires courage." Bill explained, "That's only logical. I can't see what the big thrill is about being worshipped. It seems a little egotistical." Satan laughed loudly, "Bill, you and I have a lot in common. We both like Mary and we don't like worshipping. We both like blackjack. How have you been doing?" Bill replied, "I think I'm improving. I wasn't too bad before, but now I'm much better. I win most of the time, so that's a good thing. Winning is fun, but it will be even more fun playing for big stakes." Satan responded, "Now that's the spirit. Remember to go around to all the casinos. Don't just pick on one casino, or they might start resenting you. Those casino thugs are not the type of people you want to have angry with you." Bill said, "I'll remember that. Seeing all the casinos will add some nice variety to things."

Satan poured everyone another round of wine and then said, "This will need to be the last round. Nostradamus has been here for a long time today. We need to let all of you rest for the big day tomorrow. I'm sure you'll be looking for the telescope case of Nostradamus. I don't want to hinder your progress. We really must be on our way." As they drank that next glass of wine, Satan and Nostradamus slowly faded out of view.

# Chapter Four

## A Short Death

Mary stated, "Satan was right. We need to get some sleep. Tomorrow is another big day of diving." Mary kissed her father good night and went with Bill over to the Deep Diver. They dressed for bed and went right to sleep. All the wine they had consumed was helpful in putting them to sleep quickly. In the morning, they were up at six o'clock. They started getting their gear ready for the dive. Once the sun was a little further up, they started their dive. Diving too early would have forced them to depend on artificial lighting. It was much better to have the help of the sun in locating the ship. As they swam side by side moving towards the ship, they noticed that the tropical fish looked quite beautiful in the bright sun on that clear day. Large schools of angel fish and neons swooped past them. Large groupers cruised by unimpressed with them. Suddenly a giant tiger shark appeared out of nowhere and closed in on them with a frontal attack. Mary remembered what Satan had said about shark bites. They didn't hurt much because of the adrenalin. She pointed her spear gun at the shark's head and fired. Her accuracy was amazing. The spear went right into the shark's head, piercing its brain. Other sharks quickly appeared, attracted by the blood. They quickly ate the tiger shark. Bill and Mary moved off to one side and then continued their long swim to the French ship. They went right to the hold at the bottom of the ship. They found that most of the cloth shipment had totally disintegrated. They used their bright lights to search the totally dark hold. They pried open ancient wooden chests and cabinets. Finally at the far stern of the ship, there was a tall closet door. It was the last place for them to look. They had been searching for fifteen minutes. There wasn't much time left. They used their pry bars to break open the locked doors. There on the bottom shelf of the closet was a long dark case which looked like it could be the telescope case. Mary opened it, and sure enough there was a telescope inside. Bill put it under his arm, and they returned to the Deep Diver.

When the telescope and case was on board, Mary opened the case and removed the telescope. Bill immediately noticed that there was a brass plate nailed to the top of the lid. He carefully removed the nails and pulled the plate from the lid. Pulling the plate away revealed the copper plate behind it. The copper plate was not corroded and was deeply engraved with Latin writing. They heard a helicopter nearby. It moved in close and started firing at them. Mary heard Jim yell, "Take it below. My enemies are making their move." Mary grabbed the copper plate and ran down to the galley. She hid the copper plate in the ice compartment of the refrigerator. Bill saw Jim fall overboard and knew he had been shot. Bullets were flying everywhere. In no time, all Jim's guards were killed or badly wounded. Four men dressed in black slid down a rope from the helicopter and landed on the Deep Diver. Each man wore a gas mask and tossed gas canisters all about the boat. Everyone on the boat was rendered unconscious by the gas. The men quickly searched the ship and found the copper plate in the refrigerator. They returned to the rope and were pulled back up into the helicopter. It left as quickly as it had appeared.

Twenty minutes later, Mary and Bill regained consciousness. Mary cried, "Where is dad? What happened to him?" Jim responded, "I'm sorry, he was shot and fell overboard. He's dead. I'm terribly sorry Mary." Mary buried her head in her hands and sobbed violently over her father's death. Bill put his arm around her and tried to console her. Finally Mary got control of her emotions. She told Bill, "We have to find his killers. Dad told me if I ever needed help and he wasn't around, to use his detective. The detective's card is on my dad's refrigerator. We have to get back to shore right away. I can't bring my dad back. I just want to avenge his death."

Mary went to the helm and started the engines. As quickly as possible she steered the boat back to shore. Bill drove them back to Jim's house. When they got there Mary rushed to the refrigerator and found the detective's business card magnetically attached to the refrigerator door. She called the number on the card. A voice message said, "Khalaf Mashhour will be out of his office until seven this evening. Please call at any time after seven." Mary told Bill, "He's unavailable till seven. We'll just have to wait. I just can't believe they killed my dad!" Bill stated, "We'd better go for a walk on the beach. It will relax you somewhat."

He took Mary's hand and led her to the beach. "Mary. The house is still bugged. We don't dare state our plans in the house." Mary responded, "Yes, you're right. I forgot. Where shall we go?" Bill stated, "We'd better get a room at a hotel. We can plan everything there."

They took the business card with them and returned to Kingston. Driving Jim's favorite car was exciting for Bill. It was a charcoal gray Porche. They stopped at the first nice hotel they saw. Mary said, "The Hilton will do. Dad often took me here for dinner. It's a nice place." They checked in and had the porter take their bags to the room. After looking at the room briefly, they went to the restaurant for some coffee. The restaurant wasn't too full. It was two in the afternoon, and the lunch crowd had already left. The receptionist seated them next to a large window with a view of the bay. The hotel was on a hillside that raised it up over the rest of the city. The restaurant had walls painted in a light pink. There were artificial palms here and there. It was a tasteful tropical motif. The waiter was a tall thin Jamaican with a friendly smile. He placed glasses of water on the table and asked, "What would you like today?" Bill responded, "Two coffees with cream and sugar." The waiter said, "Coming right up. Would you each like a menu?" Bill stated, "Not now. The coffee will do for now." "As you wish," said the waiter as he moved quickly to get the coffee.

Mary asked, "Who would have done this?" Bill answered, "It must be the same people who bugged the house. It has to be someone who knew Jim and was watching him." Mary said, "I think you're right. Possibly our detective will know something. He was probably informed about the bugging. Dad may have already put him to work on finding out who placed the bugs."

Mary used her cell phone to report her father's death to the police. They seemed surprisingly calm about it all. They took all her information over the phone. They said there was no need for her to come to the station. They would send a detective to gather more information. In twenty minutes the detective arrived at the restaurant and questioned them thoroughly. He apologized about the fact that there was little they could do for her, since there was no body to examine and the attackers left by helicopter. After making small talk for a short while, the detective left.

Bill said, "Our best hope is with detective Mashhour. He knew your dad and some of the details related to his life. He will know best how to handle the case." They drank several more cups of coffee and then went to their room to shower. They still were covered with the salt from the mornings dive. After they each took a shower, they spent some time in the room's hot tub. It was big enough for ten people. The room was one of the best in the hotel. It was on the tenth floor and overlooked the ocean. Mary stated, "We'd better eat. I'm not hungry, but we're going to need all the energy we can muster to go up against these tough guys who killed my dad." Bill responded, "You're right. We should eat. It will help pass the time until the detective gets back in his office. The police will take care of the other boat and get it back to shore. We don't need to worry about anything but finding the men responsible for today's attack. They must be wealthy. They were able to hire a crack team of snipers and a modern helicopter."

Mary and Bill spent the rest of the afternoon in the restaurant. When seven o'clock came, Mary called detective Mashhour on the cell phone. Mashhour's voice sounded vaguely familiar. He gave them the address of his office, which was on the west side of town, near the beach. Bill drove as quickly as he dared. Mary was anxious to get started on finding the killers. When they arrived at the door of Mashhour's office they were in for a big surprise. Mary's dad, Jim, opened the door. Mary felt herself getting a little weak in the knees. She almost fainted. "How . . . How can you still be alive?" asked Mary. Jim smiled and hugged her, "I didn't want to put you through this, Mary, but I had to convince our enemies that they had succeeded in killing me. Now they will leave me alone and I can find out who they are." Mary exclaimed, "But you fell into the water!" Jim explained, "I had a crew in a mini submarine, waiting for me. I knew the enemy would attack the minute we found the copper plate. I was counting on the two of you to be able to survive. I guess I was right." Bill scolded, "They used gas on us. It could have been lethal gas!" Jim laughed, "Satan wouldn't have allowed that to happen." Mary got a little upset, "You sure trust in him more than I do. He probably hasn't been monitoring any of this day's happenings. You were just lucky that we weren't both killed." Jim frowned, "Don't be angry with me, Mary. I had to do something to get these jerks to make a move. I'm sure I know who they are now. They aren't little fish. They launched a professional attack on us. This has to be the work of Imperial Petroleum. It's not the whole company. Just the top executives. I own a large percentage of the company, and the top execs are tired of my meddling. I know where to find these guys and I'm going after them right now."

Mary asked, "What about Bill and I. Won't you be needing some help?" Jim responded, "I've got some friends who are experienced at getting information out of people. I'll take them with me. You and Bill can direct the repair of the boats. It won't take me more than a couple days to get the copper plate back. The boats need to be ready." Mary said, "That sounds good. We'll take care of the boats. You get the copper plate back."

Bill and Mary went back to the boats and started calling businesses to repair the broken glass and the bullet damage to the boats. Jim phoned his friends and had them meet him at the airport. They were big Jamaican men with muscular builds and intimidating appearance. None of the four men looked like you would want to mess with them. Jim had learned to know them at the Kingston casino, The Flamingo. They all worked there as guards. Jim knew the owner of The Flamingo, and had arranged for them to miss work for a few days. They flew first class together with Jim. Jim had explained the situation to them over the phone and they were all eager to do their part to help Jim. In no time they were at the Blue Chip casino in Michigan City. They had taken a limo from O'Hare. Jim knew it was a favorite meeting place for Derrick Sanders, Imperial Petroleum's C.E.O. and Warren Miller, the vice president. He sent a courier to each man with a letter from the other requesting an urgent meeting. Neither man wanted to discuss their crime on the phone or by e-mail, so they had to comply with the request and meet each other in person.

When each man arrived at the room, he was frisked and swept into the room. They were both gagged and put through some Jamaican persuasion practices involving lit cigarettes. Both men swore it was the other man's idea. Derrick Sanders volunteered that the copper plate was in the trunk of his red 1962 Corvette which was on the second floor of the parking garage. He said, "The keys are in my pocket. I'll never do anything like this again. I promise." One of the guards took the keys and retrieved the copper plate. He handed it to Jim. Jim smiled to see the copper plate. Then he frowned. "We could get in trouble for torturing these two. I think I know someone who would like to meet them." Jim pulled his pentagram table cloth out of his attaché case. Then he pulled out a bottle of ganga drink from the case. He set up a table for one of his séances. Everyone drank some of the ganga drink. Black candles were set in candlesticks and lit. The lights were turned off. Jim stated, "Satan, my old friend. I have some people for you to meet. They have tried to kill me. I'm asking you to take care of them for me. If it pleases you, feel free to come and visit. If you are too busy, then please just take these two murderers off my hands." A sulfurous odor filled the room and the candles shook on the table. In an instant the two murderers disappeared. Satan's voice could be heard as he spoke and laughed, "I'll enjoy working on these men's teeth. My new dental chair and the dental drill with dull drill bits have just arrived. I'll have your two pests longing for death in no time. Ha, ha, ha-a-a!"

# Chapter Five

## The Search Continues

When Jim returned to the Kingston marina, it was noon. He found Bill and Mary putting the final touches on the repair of the two boats. All the broken glass had been repaired by professionals. Bill was applying a final coat of paint to the bullet hole repairs, while Mary continued looking for any remaining slivers of glass on the deck. She was using a vacuum sweeper to assure that no invisible slivers would find their way into bare feet. Jim stepped onto the Deep Diver, where Bill and Mary were working, and proudly displayed the copper plate. Bill got a paper and pen and started translating right away. The Latin read:

Navis Gallicusaum ferre thesaurus magnusaum
Depressus adjacere coalinas scopulus,
Septenriones centum cubitum de domus
De scriptor Ian Fleming, prope oppidum de Oracabeza.

Bill quickly and carefully wrote down the translation:

Ship French carried treasure great
Sunken adjacent to coral reef,
North 100 cubits of house
Of author Ian Fleming, near town of Oracabeza.

Jim and Mary were looking over Bill's shoulders as he wrote. Jim stated, "I'd like to go there with the two of you. I'll take my boat and stay in it most of the time. I'll let the two of you have your privacy as much as you like." Bill replied, "We'd love to have you with us." "Yes, do come and be with us!" retorted Mary. Jim responded, "I'd love to be there to see the treasure when you bring it up. There isn't much threat from pirates on that side of the island. Since so many wealthy people live around there, security is pretty good. The coast guard is well funded. It won't hurt to have The Gull close by just in case some pirates would be bold enough to go to that area. I'll hire four guards to come along. George knows some good people. I like to provide employment for some of the local people. It gives me a good name around Kingston." Mary exclaimed, "I agree. Give some of the local people good jobs. Hopefully none of them will be shot this time!" Jim lamented, "I regret that some of the men died on the last dive. I'm sending help to their families. This dive should be less eventful, I hope."

Mary explained, "I'd like for Bill and I to start off for Oracabeza in the morning. You can meet us there once you've found your guards." Jim said, "That's fine with me. I can understand how anxious you must be to start the next round of dives. Do you remember how to find Oracabeza?" Mary laughed, "Sure. You took me past it several times when I was younger and we used to tour the coastline. I have total recall for coastlines." "If you have any trouble locating it, just radio the coast guard. They'll send out a ship to help you find it. I'm friends with all of them. I'm always sending them pizza when I'm in their area. They never forget a free pizza." Mary smiled, "It's good to have lots of friends. We'll call them if we get lost."

Jim went back to The Gull and talked with the casino guards who had helped him in Michigan City. They had been relaxing on deck with some cold drinks. He pulled out his billfold and started to pull out some bills. The tallest guard, named Raul stopped him. He stated, "Mr. Valdez says this is on the house. He pays us. You just come and play at the casino often. That will make him happy." Jim smiled, "At least let me give you some of our white wine and delicious cheeses!" Raul replied, "That's good. Most gracious of you Mr. Thresher."

Jim went down to the galley and brought up a bottle of wine for each man and a large platter full of cheese. They all talked about the casino and their plans for the future. They waved as Bill and Mary pulled out from the dock with Deep Diver. While Jim had been gone, Bill and Mary had been busy getting the boat supplied with provisions as well as doing their repair work. They waved back to Jim and the guards and slowly headed for open ocean.

Jim didn't drink much wine since he knew he had to drive. He took the guards back to the casino. Once they arrived at The Flamingo, Jim located Marcos Valdez and thanked him for his generosity. They had a meal together and discussed the work the guards had done in Michigan City. Jim made sure he spoke highly of the men to their employer. After the meal, Jim went to the blackjack tables. He wanted to lose a little money to help out his friend, Valdez. He played for about an hour and only managed to break even. Finally he bet the maximum $2,500 bet on a hand and lost. Relieved that he had paid back his friend, he cashed in his chips and went to find George.

George was back at Jim's house trimming some trees. Jim walked up to him and stated, "George. I need four good men for body guards. I think the shooting is over now. I just want a little insurance against pirates. We're going to Oracabeza tomorrow. I need these people by morning. Can you do it? I'll pay them well." George laughed, "Sure Jim. I can have them ready for you first thing in the morning." Jim invited George into the house for a cup of coffee. They talked about the location of the treasure and about the happenings in Michigan City. Then George took his Toyota Corolla and went to round up his guard friends. George took them right to The Gull where Jim met him. The guards unpacked their things in their spacious crew quarters. Then the men went on deck to listen to Jim describe their new job to them. Jim showed them around the ship and trained them in their various duties. At supper time Jim took them to The Flamingo and treated them to a sumptuous meal. They all stayed up late playing blackjack. Jim tried to teach them the techniques described by Nostradamus, but the men were not in the mood to learn theory. They just wanted to play one hand at a time. *Just as well,* thought Jim. *They will lose more money to my friend Valdez.*

When the men had lost most of their money, they all went back to The Gull. Jim gave them all an advance in pay, so they wouldn't feel so bad. They all went to their bunks and got some sleep. Jim had warned them that he wanted to get an early start in the morning.

Bill and Mary arrived near Oracabeza late in the evening. They knew they would have to wait till morning to be able to spot the little town and the small coral reef that jutted up out of the water in front of Ian Fleming's house. The Fleming house was distinctive because it had a cement stairway that went down along the right side of the house and onto the beach. The house was right on a small cliff that was close to the beach. The house had unusually high windows which the author had designed with an eye towards keeping out the powerful ocean winds. He probably didn't want his papers blowing all about the house. Mary and Bill anchored down about a mile off shore. They weren't aware that they were only two miles east of

Oracabeza. They watched a James Bond movie together and ate pop corn with lots of real butter and salt on it.

When the movie was over they went to bed and quickly fell asleep. At around 2:00 o'clock in the morning there was a bright white glowing thing at the foot of their bed which caused them to wake up. They could see a six foot tall radiant female angel waiting to speak to them. They both sat up in bed and looked wide eyed at the angel. The angel spoke, "My name is Ruth. I've come to offer guidance and friendship from Jesus Christ our Lord and Savior. Satan has deceived you with lies. He says that he has wonderful times in store for you. The opposite is true. Mary, he knows that you didn't trust him and believe that he protected you from poisonous gas and bullets. He is quite angry with you. If he gets you down in hell, he will strap you in his new dental chair and drill out all of your teeth. I promise that I know what I'm talking about. You and Bill need to marry and become Christians as soon as possible. Jesus loves you, and wants you to be in heaven with him when you die. When your father Jim learns what Satan has in store for you, he will convert to Christianity as well. Satan cannot be trusted. He prides himself in how sneaky and two faced he is. His account of the Cain and Abel story was deceptive. God loved both of those men equally. He didn't force Cain to be a jealous person. Cain should have traded his vegetables for sheep and offered God an appropriate sacrifice. Vegetables don't even burn well. They just steam and char. Lamb, on the other hand, sizzles nicely on the grill and gives off a delightful aroma that humans and God alike delight in. Heaven is not a place where perpetual boring praising goes on. There is no unhappiness in heaven. All illness and injuries are cured. People thoroughly enjoy every day in heaven. And remember, even Satan had to admit that the wine in heaven is better than what he makes. Wouldn't you like to be on the winning team and drink the best wine?" Mary responded, "You've convinced me. I'll change my loyalty to Jesus, but be sure to appear to my dad. He'll never believe me if I tell him about this." Ruth replied, "I will appear to Jim. We want all of you to be together. I'm sorry that your mother will not be able to join you in heaven right away. There will be a time when she can make a choice for Jesus. Then she will join you in heaven."

Bill stated, "I believe you too. I'll become a Christian right away and we'll get married just like you said." He turned to Mary and asked, "Mary will you marry me?" Mary responded, "I will, Bill. I want to marry you right away." The angel smiled and then faded from their sight.

Jim was asleep on The Gull when the angel appeared at the right side of his bed. Jim woke slowly and realized what was beside him. He said, "I'm not dying am I?" The angel answered, "No, you are not dying soon. I want you to become a Christian. To help you decide to leave your loyalty to Satan behind, I've come with the truth about him. He plans to drill out all of Mary's teeth in his dental chair. He wants to punish her for not having enough faith in him. She didn't believe that Satan protected you from the poison gas and bullets when you were attacked at the last dive site." Jim exclaimed, "That does change things. But won't heaven be terribly boring?" The angel laughed, "Do I look terribly bored? Right before I came here, I had a glass of the best wine ever made. They only make it in heaven. If you remember, even Satan had to admit that he can't make wine as well as they make it in heaven. Wouldn't you rather have the best wine, all the time?" Jim smiled, "I know what you mean. Do you also have great cheeses?" Ruth replied, "We have the best of everything. In heaven, your life will be full of interesting travels. You will see all the wonders of the world. The new Jerusalem will settle down from heaven onto earth. The earth will become perfect. It will be more perfect than the Garden of Eden. There will be no Satan to tempt people. There will be no illness or injuries. There will be no unhappiness. You can explore the oceans the way you have in the past. There will be wonderful feasts. There will be singing. You will sincerely want to sing the praises of your Lord God and of Jesus who made your forgiveness possible. Will you become a disciple of Jesus?"

Jim laughed, "You'd be a good car salesman. You've convinced me completely. But what about Satan? Won't he seek me out for punishment? Won't he punish Mary and Bill. What about George?" Ruth responded, "God will protect them. Once you choose Jesus, Satan cannot touch you. You are protected by God." Jim said, "I'll get baptized tomorrow, first thing." Ruth exclaimed, "Tomorrow might be too late. Satan was quite fond of you. He'll be enraged when he learns of your switching to Christianity. I'd better baptize you right now, if that's fine with you." Jim responded, "Sure. Let me get dressed."

Ruth waited on deck while Jim got dressed. Jim quickly pulled on a pair of jeans and rushed up to the deck. He and Ruth walked briskly to the beach and waded into the water. No one was awake at that time of the night. They were alone in the water. The angel said, "I baptize you in the name of the Father." She gently pushed Jim forward under the water. "And the Son." She submersed him again. "And the Holy Spirit." She submersed him for the last time. The Holy Spirit entered into Jim and started protecting him.

Jim asked, "Can you baptize George tonight too. Satan liked George quite a bit. He'll be mad when he finds that George has converted. George will need the protection of the Holy Spirit." Ruth stated, "We can go visit George together." They hopped in Jim's car, after he changed clothes, and went to see George. Jim called ahead on his cell phone. George woke up and answered. Jim said, "I have someone that I need for you to meet tonight. Get dressed and we'll be there in about fifteen minutes." George got dressed and waited for Jim to arrive. When George opened the door for them he was surprised to see the white glowing angel. Jim explained, "This is Ruth. She has come to offer us a better way. She says that Satan is waiting to torture Mary for not being faithful enough to him. Listen closely to Ruth." "I'm listening, Jim. I have great respect for those of the supernatural. This surely must be an angel. She glows like a light bulb." Ruth laughed, "You are right, George. I am an angel. I've come to take you from Satan's power. He has deceived everyone. He allows you to heal some people of their illnesses, but when they die, the illness will return. The way of Satan is a way of suffering. I offer you God's forgiveness. When you become a Christian you can still be a healer. God will help you. Your people will stay healed. When they die, there will be nothing but happiness in God's wonderful heaven. There will be no suffering, illness or injuries. There will be all the best wine and food. Feasting and companionship will prevail. The world will be made perfect when the New Jerusalem is lowered onto earth. You will be allowed to see the entire world and all the wonders thereof. The Holy Spirit will move you to win your friends to Jesus. Jesus made it possible for your sins to be forgiven when he died on the cross. His blood was shed to win your salvation from sin. Will you join Jim in Christianity, and be baptized tonight?"

"What about Satan. He's very powerful. He will want revenge against me!" Ruth stated, "God is more powerful. He will send his Holy Spirit to protect you. Nothing can hurt you when God is on your side." George smiled, "I want to be with Jim. He's always right. I know that an angel wouldn't lie to me. I'll be baptized. When do we go?" Ruth said, "We can go right away." Jim drove them back to the beach and George was baptized at the same spot where Jim had been baptized. They all drove back to George's house, and George changed into some dry clothes.

Ruth stated, "You'll need to start reading the Bible on a regular basis. It contains all you need to know about your new faith. I'll go through some of the basics with you now. You need to do your best to follow the Ten Commandments. Be sure to have no other gods before you. That means not calling on Satan for favors. All your allegiance must be given to Jesus. You will want to be generous with the poor. Love your neighbor as yourself. Start out by reading the New Testament. The first book, Matthew, is exceptionally good at conveying the way Jesus thought. It contains many parables of Jesus, the stories he used to show how people should live and think."

George asked, "What if I make some mistakes and sin?" Ruth smiled, "As long as you are sorry for you sin and pray for forgiveness, you will be forgiven. As a Christian you can feel friendly to Jesus. You needn't live in fear of him. He is your friend as well as your God. Jesus and his father are both to be prayed to and worshipped. Together with the Holy Spirit, they form the most powerful spiritual entity in the universe. They are more powerful than Satan and will eventually destroy him. They are allowing him to continue to exist so that people can freely choose between good and evil. Once God becomes too tired of knowing about how much evil is in the world, he will harvest the good people for heaven. The evil people will be burned in everlasting fire."

Jim asked, "What about my wife, Jeanie?" Ruth explained, "I'm not sure of all the details about that. At the end of time, though, all souls will have one final chance to choose Jesus. That is when I think you will be reunited with Jeanie. Jeanie was never presented with the chance to choose Jesus. She was not evil. She died early and did little sinning. She was only unfortunate enough to never hear about Jesus. Only God knows just how things will happen at the end of time on earth as we know it. I know he will rule justly with all souls. That's enough information for now. Be sure to read your Bibles and pray to Jesus and God every day. Jim, you'll need to get back to sleep. Next week is going to be a big week. Mary and Bill are getting baptized. Also, Bill proposed marriage to Mary tonight. She accepted, and they will be getting married quite soon. I must go now. May God bless both of you." The angel faded from sight.

Jim went back to his house and got a good night's sleep. In the morning he asked George to pick up four guards to work with them on the boat. George picked up his friends and met Jim at the boat. As George started steering The Gull into open water, Jim explained to the four new men what their duties would be. Jim stated, "I'll have a schedule of your duties posted later today. You will all take turns being cook, dishwasher and other duties which come up. Keep your guns handy. You'll be protecting a large treasure of gems, gold and silver. The area we're going to, near Oracabeza, is not prone to piracy, but we need to be sure. So I want you to stay alert. Keep an eye out across the waters in all directions." The men asked some questions about their work and Jim helped them understand what he wanted them to do in various situations. Jim asked about their families and tried his best to be a friendly understanding supervisor. One of the biggest and tallest men, Manuel, mentioned, "We all heard that some of the previous guards were killed and the rest injured. Can you tell us a little more about the dangers we'll be facing?" Jim smiled, "Your concern is understandable. We were attacked by a professional hit team that was trying to kill me and possibly my daughter. I'll be perfectly candid with you. My daughter, Mary, her fiancé Bill and I were protected by Satan. That's the only reason we are alive.

Since then I have been visited by an angel who convinced me to become a Christian. The angel will be watching over me. Mary and Bill will soon be baptized. I'm sure the angel will watch over them too. I'm not saying that we could not be killed if we are not cautious. I do think we will be helped. If we are killed we will go to heaven. That is the important thing. They have all the best wine in heaven. And excellent cheeses too." The men looked impressed. Manuel stated, "I always heard that heaven was just a bunch of harp playing and singing. You say they have the best wine?" Jim explained, "When I was friends with Satan, we had a party, and he lamented that even though he can make great wine, it isn't as good as the wine they have in heaven." Manuel said, "We have all been depending on Voodoo to save us from harm. George always used it to help us with sickness. What does George think about your Christianity?" Jim explained, "The angel appeared to George too. The angel was named Ruth. She baptized both of us last night and taught us about Christianity." Jim explained all the things the angel had said to him and then left the men alone for awhile. He went to talk to George.

While Jim discussed things with George, Manuel spoke to his friends, Paul, Matt and Juan. "If George is Christian now, we've got no Voodoo doctor to call on. We need this angel to help us. Guns alone won't save us from pirates. I think we need God's protection." stated Manuel. Paul replied, "You right about that. Jim is a nice guy, but he knows how to attract trouble. He helped the families of those dead guards, but that won't bring them back. They're still dead." Juan agreed, "I think we'd better get baptized too." "Me too." exclaimed Matt. "I don't want to end up like those other guards. Let's ask Jim how we can get baptized right away. He said we just need to be generous to the poor, read the Bible and obey the Ten Commandments. That doesn't sound too hard to do."

They all went to talk to Jim. They found him at the helm, talking to George. Manuel spoke for the group, "We want to be Christians too. This is dangerous work and we want God's protection. If we get killed we want to end up where the fun is, in heaven." Jim smiled and said, "We can get you baptized just as soon as we get to Oracabeza. We'll get their late this evening. We can find a preacher and get you all baptized the first thing in the morning. Remember though, you can't keep using the Voodoo. That would anger God and remove his protection." "We won't use Voodoo. We promise." said Manuel. The others all agreed too. Manuel shouted to George, "Can't you make this tub go any faster?" "I'll pour the coals to her." George exclaimed and pushed forward on the throttle. The boat surged ahead at full speed. They pulled up next to Deep Diver just after sun set.

Jim explained to Mary and Bill about the crew wanting to be baptized. They took the Dingy to shore and located a preacher in Oracabeza who would help them. He also agreed to do the marriage ceremony. He said he needed a couple of days to get enough people together for the marriage. It wouldn't be right without all the church people there. They needed time to prepare food and decorate the church. Bill and Mary went along with his desire to have the wedding on Saturday. It was Wednesday, so they only had to wait two more days.

# Chapter Six

## The Wedding

Preacher Roberto Hernandez, notified all the church people about the wedding, scheduled for 11:00 o'clock in the morning on Saturday. A local seamstress made up a nice veil and dress for Mary. It took two days with lots of help to make the dress. With great pride the seamstress took the dress over to the church. The church building was small and quite ancient. It was made of brick which had been painted over with white paint. There was a steeple which had a large bell. Roberto always had the bell rung on Sunday morning to announce that the service would soon be starting. When Saturday arrived he had the bell rung before the wedding. It was loud and majestic. Two hours before the wedding Roberto was having a conversation with one of his congregation members, Juanita Alvarez. He stated proudly, "Thursday morning I baptized four men from Kingston. Today I have this wedding. I am a busy man, lately!" "You are indeed busy!" replied Juanita. "Who were the men you baptized?" Roberto answered, "They are guards for the boat of Jim Thresher, the father of the bride." "It is wonderful that those men all found Jesus. Did you give them Bibles?" asked Juanita. "Yes, I gave them each a Bible. Even though they aren't from around here, they deserve a free Bible. It is essential for them to develop in their faith." Juanita asked, "Is it true that the bride and groom are going to be baptized right after their wedding?" Roberto responded, "Yes, it is true. They are eager to get things done quickly. They are going to do some treasure diving in this area. They need to finish with the wedding and baptism so they can start scuba diving." Juanita continued, "I don't want you to ask them, but they must be wealthy." "They are living on large boats directly out from the house of Ian Fleming. Even if they are renting the boats, they would need quite a bit of money." said Roberto. "Jim Fletcher paid me in advance for the wedding service. He paid much more than I asked for. He is a generous man!"

As Roberto and Juanita continued talking, the body guards along with Jim, Mary and Bill, were studying the Bible on The Gull. They were studying the Sermon on the Mount. Bill read it aloud and then prayed with his new friends and family. "Dear Lord Jesus. Thank you for giving us these wise words. It is good to know that those who morn will be comforted in heaven. Those who thirst for righteousness will be filled. In heaven there will be justice and happiness. We are glad to know that we can look forward to an afterlife that will be rewarding and interesting. Please watch over us and protect us as we search for the lost treasure of Nostradamus. We are not seeking wealth. You have already blessed us beyond imagination in that way. We only seek to experience the beauty of the treasure. If we do receive anything for the treasure, we will use it to help the poor. Amen."

Bill stated, "That was a good prayer, Jim. I have one concern. I was hoping to have some financial gain from the treasure. I need to be able to help support Mary and be the head of the household. I can't just let you and Mary pay for everything for the rest of my life." Jim laughed, "I know how you feel Bill. You'll have plenty of time to show how you can earn money later. Right now I'd like to announce that I'm offering to buy out you and Mary with regards to the Nostradamus treasure. I am confident we will find it. I want to create a museum in Oracabeza. It will help the town to thrive with tourists. Jamaica will want to claim the treasure anyway, since it is in their territorial waters. I don't want a law suit over the treasure, so I'd like to donate it to Oracabeza. I will give Mary and you each a billion dollars for your share. It will be a combined buy out and wedding gift." Bill exclaimed, "I know I accept. You are quite generous." Mary chimed in, "I accept too. It's a wonderful wedding gift." Jim continued, "There are Christian missionaries working here in Jamaica. I am going to help them financially as well. Ruth, the angel said we need to help the poor. I intend to do just that."

Mary asked, "You aren't going to give away all your money, are you?" "No." replied Jim. "I'm going to keep much of my money so I can make more money. I'm selling my oil stock. That company reminds me too much of the executives who tried to have us killed. I'm going to invest in green technologies. I feel that is where the profits of the future are. I also want to start a company that will drill into the hot rocks near Yosemite Park. That area is seething with energy just waiting to be harnessed. I'll go just out of the park area and drill down into the hot rocks to generate steam for electric generators. Some say that whole area is about to blow sky high, but I'm betting it won't happen until we're all in heaven. My company will net billions of dollars in profits before the area blows up. Greenland is already using this type of geothermal energy to power its country. I love being on the cutting edge of developments. It's exciting. With the profits from geothermal energy sales, I can do much to feed a hungry world."

Bill stated, "Mary and I can start our own companies now. I like the geothermal idea. The center of the earth is so hot and big, we would never run the risk of cooling it off too much. It is a constant source of heat energy. We could bore into the base of Mt. St. Helens and use that heat to generate steam." Mary added, "The volcanoes of Hawaii are untapped as energy sources. The whole state could easily be powered by steam from volcano heat. If we become major suppliers of steam generated electricity, we'll be able to make unbelievable profits. Like dad said, 'We can do much to feed a hungry world.' I like the idea of helping the poor and hungry people of the world."

Manuel said, "I'd like to start a lumber business. With God on my side, I'm sure I could succeed. I just need a loan so I can buy some equipment. I would plant ten trees for every one that I cut. Many companies aren't planting trees at all. Large numbers of trees are lost to illegal loggers who steal trees from our national forest preserves. I want to work legally and beneficially." Jim replied, "You can count on me to loan you some money. I like the idea of you planting lots of trees. Where ever an area is opened up by your logging, you can fill it back in with new trees. I hope that by providing cheap electricity for people to heat their homes with, I'll be making it so people don't cut so many trees for firewood. There are so many people being driven to heating with wood, that I fear for the continued existence of enough trees in America. Countries like Haiti have used up most of their trees for cooking fires and the sale of charcoal. If they had cheap electricity, the pressure on wood for cooking, would be reduced. Haiti has no hot rocks close to the surface. Wind powered generators or wave powered generators would be good for them. Solar would also be good for a country like Haiti with no hot rocks to tap into."

Matt volunteered, "I too would like to start a business. I think Jamaica should have wind power. I'd like to start a wind power company." Jim stated, "I believe in you Matt. I'll make sure you get some money to work with. The world needs more Christian businessmen like you." Each guard thought of a business to start. Jim promised them all financial support.

Bill and Mary started getting the dive equipment ready. They wanted to start diving the next day after their wedding. Jim went to the galley with Matt and Manuel. He showed them how he liked his sausage cooked. They prepared a meal of pancakes and sausage for everyone. The crew all sat down to the meal which was supplemented with plenty of orange juice. Jim said grace and then they all started eating. After breakfast Jim explained to the crew, "We are having a wedding today in Oracabeza. We'd like all of you to attend." The men all agreed to go. The small dingy had to make two trips to get them all to land. They made it to the church in plenty of time for Mary to put on her dress. It was a bright sunny day. A slight breeze was waving the leaves of the palm trees which surrounded the church. The church had a nicely trimmed small green yard. Many people were still standing outside talking. There was still a half hour till the service would begin. Many children were playing in the yard. There was laughter and shouting. Everyone was having a good time. Mary waited inside the church for the service to start. Jim introduced Bill to people outside the church. They all wanted to meet him.

Finally 11:00 o'clock arrived and everyone was seated inside the church. The organ began to play and the wedding proceeded without a hitch. The couple took their vows and exchanged rings. Finally after some words about the importance of marriage, Roberto invited Bill to kiss his bride. After the kiss and the wedding was complete, Bill and Mary got dressed for the baptism. It came right after the wedding. They were baptized in the ocean, not far from the house of Ian Fleming. When the baptism was finished, there was a big feast. All the church people had brought food with them, and there was a hog that had been roasting all morning. The food and celebration lasted all afternoon. The people were all dressed in bright pastels of blue, pink and yellow. The men were dressed in their best fancy shirts, which were heavily embroidered. They sat at picnic tables under the palm trees and ate till they were full. They continued talking and joking around for most of the afternoon. The people were really enjoying themselves. Mary was delighted to see they were all so happy. She hugged her new husband and whispered something in his ear. He smiled and walked her to the beach where the dingy was waiting. Jim and the crew would keep the party going till late at night, while Bill and Mary enjoyed a quick honeymoon on the Deep Diver. After many hours of passionate love making, they showered and dressed. Laughing and happy, they motored the dingy back to the beach to pick up some of the crew. In no time everyone was back on the boats. Late in the morning, they would be making their first dive on the north side of the coral reef in front of Ian Fleming's house. It was right where the Nostradamus copper plate had said it would be. There was little wind and the ocean was calm. Mary and Bill fell asleep quickly in each other's arms.

# Chapter Seven

## Ian Fleming's Coral Reef

The morning sunrise brought with it calm waters. There was only a slight breeze rippling the surface of the ocean. Mary and Bill were up early preparing their equipment for the dive. Mary trained Manuel on how to operate the dive radio. He was to warn her if any troubles were developing around the boats. The communication would be one way. Mary would not be able to speak well with the air supply mouth piece in her mouth. At least she and Bill would know if they needed to come up early from their dive. Once Manuel felt comfortable operating the radio, Mary checked the air regulators on their tanks. They were operating properly. Bill helped her get the fins, weighted dive belts and other equipment organized and ready to use. Jim helped them put new batteries in their metal detectors. The detectors were a special variety designed to withstand the rigors of being submersed in salt water at depths up to three hundred feet. The ocean bottom was only eighty feet down near the base of the coral reef. As you went north into open ocean, the bottom dropped off dramatically to depths over two hundred feet.

When it was eleven o'clock, the sun was at a high enough level that visibility would be good at the base of the coral reef. Mary and Bill quickly helped each other put on their air tanks and lead belts. Manuel made on last test of the radio, and then Bill and Mary jumped off the rear of Deep Diver. They descended slowly to the ocean bottom, kicking in a leisurely fashion with their fins. The water was light blue in color. Small colorful tropical fish were plentiful. A large school of black and white angel fish were following them down to the sandy bottom. On the bottom were some large groupers and a school of red snapper. In the distance were some hammerhead sharks. They appeared uninterested and didn't move any closer. They were only black silhouettes in the distance. Mary and Bill arrived quickly at the bottom. The descent had caused their ears to pop once or twice, but there was no real discomfort. The sun was bright enough to light up the sandy bottom and make it appear to be a creamy white color. There were many sand dollars and star fish crawling ever so slowly along the bottom.

The coral reef was a collage of red, purple, white and yellow. Small striped neons darted in and out from amongst the various coral formations. Some of the corals looked like human brains, and were a cream color. The brilliant red corals stuck out most predominately. They were a branching coral that resembled thin tree limbs in their growth patterns. At the base of the coral reef was much thick steaming vegetation. There were prominent outcroppings of rock to the north of the coral reef. Mary thought to herself, *No wonder the ship went down when it got in close to this reef. The rock outcroppings would have ripped the belly right out of the ship. The treasure should be somewhere close to these rock outcroppings.*

She signaled to Bill to start using his metal detector. They started scanning the area all around the base of the tall rock formations. Finally they got a strong signal midway between the rock formation and the coral reef. The rock formation was a hundred feet north of the coral reef. They started digging eagerly with their hand trowels. Before they located anything, they started running out of air. Mary left her lead belt at the spot to mark the location. Slowly they returned to the surface.

Jim and Manuel helped them up the ladder once they were at the surface. Next they helped Bill and Mary get their air tanks off. Jim asked, "Did you find anything?" Bill exclaimed, "We got some intense signals from one location midway between some high rock outcroppings and the coral reef." Mary butted in, "We dug down almost two feet and then started to run out of air. We need to use double tanks so we can stay down longer." Jim responded, "We have plenty of double tanks. I don't think we'll run out. How deep did the metal detector say the metal was?" Bill answered, "Between three and four feet. We should be able to dig down that deep in just a day or two." "He's right." agreed Mary. "If the weather stays good, it shouldn't take us long to find out what we've detected."

The next day was calm again, with a slight breeze out of the west. Mary and Bill were in the water by nine in the morning. It was a little more difficult to see that early, since the sun wasn't directly over head. Still it wasn't difficult to find where they had been digging. They renewed their efforts and dug with enthusiasm. Curious parrot fish and groupers kept swimming by close to them. The fish were so close the divers could have touched them. One large nurse shark swam by close to the bottom. It meant them no harm. It, like the other fish, was only curious. Mary's arms grew tired. She stopped for a moment to watch the fish and look around. The water was of a slightly deeper blue at that time of day. She hadn't noticed before how many sponges and corals grew in clumps near the base of the coral reef. She was delighted that this area was unspoiled by pollution. She hoped it would always stay like this. She wanted to return often. Her arms started to feel a little better, and she felt guilty watching Bill work alone. She dug in with renewed enthusiasm. Finally, after about forty minutes their tanks were running low on air. They had been down a little longer than they should have been. Bill led the way as they ascended back up to Deep Diver.

After resting for four hours, they went back down to the dig sight. They dug at a fast pace and finally hit something metallic. In another twenty minutes, they could see they had discovered a cannon. It was made of brass and was worth a lot of money, but it wasn't what they were looking for. They returned to Deep Diver with the bad news. Once they were back on the boat, Mary lamented, "It was only a blasted cannon. All that digging!" Jim frowned, "You can't expect to find the treasure instantly! Half the fun is in the search." Bill added, "The cannon's worth lots of money. We just don't have time for it right now. We can pick it up later. Now we need to get back to work with the metal detectors." Mary told her dad, "If we found a cannon, the treasure must be close by!" Jim reassured her, "You're right. It should be near the cannon. I think the ship was so badly smashed that all the wood was washed away by the waves. We can try again tomorrow."

That evening they went to the beach and had a bonfire with the church people. There was much Bible reading and singing of Christian songs. It went on well into the night. The stars and moon were out. It was a cloudless night and a great time to be out on the beach with friends.

That night Satan was having a conversation with Nostradamus:

Satan: Mary Thresher and her friends have double crossed me. If she hadn't shown great doubt in my ability to protect her, the angel never would have come to win her over. She was the weak link. Everyone else followed the angel after Mary was won over. I'm thinking on what to do to her. Do you have any ideas, Nostradamus? Don't you agree that she is unworthy to find your treasure?

Nostradamus: She's intelligent and aggressive. That would qualify her for the treasure. Too bad she has become a Christian. I would prefer that someone else would find the treasure. She has an angel protecting her. I'm not sure what we can do. Can you give them bad weather? Maybe churn up the seas and sink her boat that way?

Satan: Of course I can churn up the seas. It will be impossible to kill her with her angel watching over her, but at least we can make life miserable for her.

Satan laughed diabolically as he contemplated his next move against Mary Thresher and her people. He consoled himself by reminding Nostradamus of how evil most humans are.

Satan: Even if I don't succeed in stopping Mary Thresher, I am succeeding with the majority of humans. They eagerly allow me to fill their hearts with malice. They yell wildly at each other and stress each other out. Bosses degrade and humiliate their poor underlings. That's the sort of thing that warms my heart. I'll have fun with those egotistical bosses when I get them. I'll drill every one of their teeth out. Then I'll put them under the supervision of many of the people they humiliated. They will be made to clean the foul smelling floors all around hell. They will learn the true meaning of humiliation.

Nostradamus: There is a certain undeniable justice in what you are saying, most intelligent one. There are certain types of people who cannot handle power. They become sadistic persecutors of the people they supervise.

Satan: I may not get all the quality people, but no one can deny that I receive by far the most people. People are naturally evil. They don't like hard work. They long to get something for nothing. Thievery is on the rise. Illegal drugs are helping me make murder and bank robbing a way of life for thousands of people in the world. War is on my side. There are always people who want to start wars or aggravate them. Some of the most intelligent people in the world are promoting the idea that any god will do. Just so you believe in a supreme being. I love those people. What a beautiful way to have other gods before you! A delightful disregard for one of the Ten Commandments!

Nostradamus: You seem to be firmly in charge of things. The Christians do not have firm control of the world. The evil people of the world are pushing things in the direction you would approve of. I don't fully understand why you punish almost all people, whether they are for you or not.

Satan: They are all humans. I detest them because they are inferior. They are not angels like I am. They are weak and ineffective. They are stupid. They have a chance for heaven and a happy utopia. They choose evil. They prove that I was right about humans all along. God created them thinking they would be nice companions who would respect him and worship him. All he got for his trouble was a massive quantity of disrespectful unrepentant sinners. He'll have to burn most of them with me in the eternal fiery pit.

Nostradamus: That does seem a bit futile. How could God have made such a mistake?

Satan: Who can know the mind of God? He must get such a thrill out of one repentant sinner, that it makes all the trouble worth while.

Jesus keeps annoying me by arranging for the forgiveness of some of my most promising sinners. Just when I think I'm going to get someone down here with some backbone and a creative mind, they get side tracked by Jesus. He's a force to be reckoned with. I'm not looking forward to Armageddon. That final battle will be my undoing. Just as my forces are closing in on Jerusalem, fire will come down from God and destroy us all.

Nostradamus: You certainly know your Bible!

Satan: I study the parts that affect me. I know I'll be thrown into the eternal fiery pit. I just need to contemplate how to give the most trouble to humans and God, during the time I have left. Why don't we have some wine and cheese tonight, Nostradamus? There will be plenty of time to churn up the ocean tomorrow. I'll wait till Mary and her husband are down under the ocean and close to uncovering the treasure. I love to snatch things away from people just when they think they are in possession of them. Mary's heartbreak will be a great consolation to me. I really despise that young woman!

Nostradamus: She double crossed you and broke her promise to be your friend. You are justified in hating her. Let's have that wine and cheese you spoke of. Don't let the thought of her ruin your evening!

Satan: Well spoken, Nostradamus. You are a sage counselor. That's why I keep you around!

Satan made the wine and cheese appear on a table before them. They sat and enjoyed large quantities of both.

Nostradamus: It's hard to imagine any wine better than this. You do excellent work, oh god of light. You are truly enlightened! After you finish that slice of cheese, will you tell me some of your plans for the future? I'm sure they would entertain me.

Satan: I fly by the seat of my pants. Where ever I see a good place to cause temptation, I move in. I especially love tempting powerful people in high places. When the evening news showcases how some politician has been bribed of been caught in sexual scandal, it makes me feel more powerful. Everyone can see that I am in charge. I love it when unusual people are harassed and ridiculed by surrounding people until that person snaps and takes out revenge on the people who think they are so much better. That kind of intense rage unleashed on the deserving and undeserving, makes me feel warm all over!

Nostradamus: Once again I must comment on your impeccable sense of justice. So often harassment goes unpunished. If it weren't for good lawyers there would hardly ever be any punishment for harassment. What do you think of lawyers?

Satan: They have there place. Some please me. Others annoy me. I wish there would be more lawyers suing doctors. It bothers me that so many people are cured of great illnesses. One of my people shoots some preacher in the heart and a clever doctor repairs him. They snatch victory right out of my clutches!

Nostradamus: What about the environment? What will you be doing in that area?

Satan: I don't need to do too much. There will always be plenty of people who love to cut down all the trees without planting any. It's much more cost effective for cities to let sewage flow into rivers, than to totally revamp the water and sewage draining systems. Rivers will always be polluted even without my intervention. I'm foreseeing radioactive pollution of high concentration. I will help it along of course. By firing up the anger of world leaders, I can bring about many nuclear wars. The radiation will fill the oceans and rivers. Humans and animals alike, will become mutated. It's easy to stop certain types of pollution, but atomic radiation stays around for a long long time. The destruction of the human gene pool will warm the cockles of my heart. When people can no longer think properly or feed themselves, this will delight me. I only hope they are not all destroyed. I need millions of them for the final battle. I can't charge up against Jerusalem alone. I need my evil hordes to help kill off the Christians and Jews.

Nostradamus: The future is complex, I can see. Perhaps I've had a little too much wine. I feel a little confused. You want mankind destroyed, yet you need millions of them for the final battle. That appears to be a dilemma.

Satan: I'll find a way to make it work out! Have some more wine. It's low in alcohol content. Everyone gets to feeling a little lost when I try to map out the future for them. Have you ever read the Book of Revelation? Now that's a little confusing at times. I suppose I'm not meant to understand it perfectly. I get the main ideas though. The evil people will eventually be punished, and the righteous will be rewarded. That sounds logical. I just wish I was the winner.

They continued on for hours discussing all facets of the future and consuming copious quantities of wine and cheese.

The next day, Mary and Bill detected another concentration of metal. They dug for an hour until they were getting low on air. They removed enough sand to allow them to view the top few inches of a square golden box with heavy metal support straps. It appeared to be the treasure. They were quite excited and returned to the boat as rapidly as they dared.

Four hours later they had waited long enough to go down again. Mary exclaimed, "I can't believe we've actually located the treasure. This has to be it." Bill stated, "We shouldn't count our chickens before they're hatched.

You could be giving us bad luck by talking like that." Mary laughed, "Don't talk about bad luck. We're Christians now. Our angel will protect us." Bill smiled, "Our angel may be a busy angel. I just hope she isn't preoccupied if we need her." Mary frowned, "Can't you have a little more faith. Faith is important. I didn't have faith in Satan, but I think that was just good instincts. His promises seemed a little too good to believe." "I'll try to have more faith." promised Bill.

Jim said, "You'd better take the rope and basket with you this time. It sounds like you've just about completely uncovered the treasure. Take this pry bar for the lid. You'll need to bring the treasure up little by little. The chest will be too heavy to lift when it's full of treasure."

Mary and Bill descended slowly with the basket and rope. The basket was six feet by six feet, and made of stainless steel mesh. It drooped in the middle to allow things to be placed on it with no fear of them rolling off. Just as they were getting close to the treasure, Mary got a call on her radio. "Return to the surface, quick. Bad storm!" Bill and Mary hurried back to the boat. The wind was howling and the waves were high. Jim shouted, "A sudden gale has hit us from out of nowhere. The weather radio gave us no warning about this." With great difficulty, Bill and Mary managed to get back on the boat. The winds were exceeding seventy miles per hour. Waves were climbing to twenty feet or more. Lightning was flashing all around the boats. Jim shouted, "We'd better all get below deck before we get hit by lightening." They quickly climbed down the stairs to the galley of Deep Diver.

"How could a storm come up so quickly?" asked Mary. "Do you think someone is working against us?" Jim exclaimed, "It would be just like Satan to pick a time like this for revenge." They were all tossed about in the galley. Jim prayed silently and eagerly for the angel to appear. Suddenly a white light appeared before them. Quickly it turned into the shape of their guardian angel. Ruth asked them, "What is it? Why have you called for me?" Jim stated, "I think Satan is causing this storm. Would you please save us from his wrath? I know you are capable. Ruth drew a sword from her belt and disappeared instantly.

She reappeared before Satan and ordered him to stop causing the storm. Satan laughed and said, "God sends a woman to boss me around? Why should I listen to you?" He laughed diabolically. Ruth pointed her sword at Satan's new dental chair. It disappeared. Satan gasped, "What have you done with my chair. I use it to punish evil. That is what God wants me to do. Bring it back." Ruth explained, "Stop the storm and I will bring back your dental chair." Satan cursed a vile curse and caused the storm to stop. His chair reappeared at once. Satan yelled, "Now be gone and do me no more harm!" Ruth stated, "Leave Jim and his group alone and I will leave you alone." Satan frowned but reluctantly stated, "Agreed. Come here no more!" Ruth returned to heaven.

Now that the seas were calm, Jim and his group all gave praise to God for helping them. They began another dive right away. The sun was bright and there was only a slight breeze. Bill and Mary made their way back to the treasure chest. It was almost completely covered with sand from the storm. They dug at the sand for almost an hour. Finally, when half of the chest was uncovered, they pried open the lid with a pry bar. The treasure was even more amazing than they had anticipated. Large gems were on top. There were diamonds and rubies as large as your fist. There were several gem covered crowns and chalices. Never had such an amazing treasure been uncovered. Not in the history of the world. They carefully placed the large gems, crowns and chalices in the basket. Next they pulled heavy gold chains with gold crosses out of the treasure chest. They placed these in the basket as well. They loaded about a fourth of the contents of the chest into the basket. Bill jerked on the rope to signal for the crew to bring the basket to the surface. Slowly and carefully the crew winched the basket to the surface. Bill and Mary followed it to the surface. Once to the surface Mary pulled back her mask and yelled, "We found it. This is only a fourth of it. These must be the favorite things of King Henry II. I've never seen such valuable treasure! I can't believe it!" "It's amazing!" responded Jim. "We'll have a very popular museum with all these fabulous items."

They carefully unloaded the basket and then spent the day bringing up the rest of the treasure. It took them the rest of the week to finish digging up the golden chest itself. They had to wrap nylon webbed straps around it and pull it up with a steel cable. It weighed almost a thousand pounds. That much gold was worth over a hundred million dollars at the time. The guards stayed on constant watch for pirates. Jim guided the boats into the harbor at Montego Bay, where he called in the Jamaican authorities to take over protection of the treasure. He told them about his plans for a Museum.

Jim's old friend, Roberto Vasquez was in charge of the Montego Bay police department. When Roberto arrived he shook Jim's hand with enthusiasm. "You and your daughter have done a fine thing. To give such a treasure to the city, will bring many tourists and help with our economy." Jim explained, "Bill and Mary found the treasure. We could have never brought it up from the ocean bottom without the help of our guardian angel, Ruth." Roberto laughed, "Yes, we all have guardian angels. We must always thank God for our good fortune." Roberto had his most trusted men secure the treasure at the Banco Central. The central bank was well guarded and capable of ensuring the safety of the treasure until the museum could be built. Roberto treated Jim, Mary, Bill and the crew to a hog roast on a nearby beach. There was singing and dancing. As the sun started to set, Mary sighed and whispered to Bill, "Now we can enjoy our honeymoon the way it should be." Bill smiled and responded, "I think we should honeymoon in Australia. I hear the Great Barrier Reef is one of the greatest sights in the world. The reefs there are still pristine and full of color and life." "I wasn't actually talking about diving." stated Mary. "However I like your idea. We can find the solitude I was referring to also. Some remote island is what I had in mind." Bill laughed, "I'm sorry Mary. I long to be alone with you too, in some nice romantic spot. We can stay there as long as we want."

Bill and Mary flew first class to Cairns, Australia and started their honeymoon with an evening on the beach in a first class bungalow. The weather was warm and calm as they walked along the white sandy beach. The flight had been a long one, but they had been able to sleep much of the time. Just as the flight was ending, they had tanked up on strong coffee. Now they were wide awake and walked slowly for miles as they discussed their plans for the future. The newlyweds were hand in hand as they walked under the golden colors of the setting sun. Mary spoke softly, "I wish we could spend the night on a blanket on the beach like we did in Jamaica." "We can rent a bungalow on a secluded island." responded Bill. "We only have our current bungalow for a week. I was hoping we could get our dive boat selected this week and buy some equipment. I don't like putting a regulator mouth piece in my mouth after someone else has been diving with it." Mary responded, "I agree we need our own equipment. I don't want to dive on a boat with dozens of other divers stirring up the silt and sand on the bottom. There are certain to be dive boats and crews for hire to individuals." Bill said softly, "We might as well buy a boat. That way we can hire exactly the type of people we want to have working for us." Mary agreed, "Yes. I keep forgetting that we have so much money. Our own boat would be much nicer. We can hire an excellent cook and some housekeepers. I want us to have plenty of time to relax together. A vacation like this can turn into too much work if we aren't careful. After we spend a few days here honeymooning, we'll buy a boat and hire a crew. We can enjoy a remote island for a couple weeks and then start diving from our own boat."

The sun was now down as Bill and Mary filled out the details of their plans. The moon and stars came out. It was a perfectly clear night with not even the slightest breeze blowing. The newly weds stopped a few hundred yards from their bungalow and kissed each other with passion. The moon and stars reminded them of their night on the beach together in Jamaica. Realizing they weren't alone on the beach, they rushed to their bungalow and allowed their passions to unfurl. After they had fully sated their desires, Mary stated, "I'm hungry. We forgot to eat supper." Bill smiled, "I'm hungry too. Some of the restaurants around here serve full meals around the clock. We can find one on the beach where there's a view of the water."

They had rented a Toyota Corolla at the airport. Bill consulted with the concierge of the bungalow complex. They hopped into the car and started a leisurely drive along the beach to the south. Only a mile down the road, was the restaurant which the concierge had recommended. The restaurant was at the top of The Conch hotel. Bill parked in the hotel parking garage and they took the elevator to the top of the hotel. The restaurant was still busy. Bill asked the hostess for a seat by the ocean. There was still one available. They watched with pleasure as yachts moved slowly through the darkness. Mary ordered first, when the waitress appeared. "I'll have the prime rib, well done, and mashed potatoes with beef gravy." Bill said, "I'll take the same, but medium well." Mary asked for a side order of fried butterfly shrimp. She apologized, "I'm really hungry." For drinks, they contented themselves with the water provided at the table.

Mary said with a sigh, "I hope we can find a remote island with short notice. We didn't plan this ahead very well." "The high end retreats are probably not fully booked." responded Bill. "I'm sure we can find something quite nice, although it will be expensive. This is our honeymoon, after all. This is no time to economize."

While they waited on the food, Bill phoned the concierge and asked him to book them a week on a totally private island. Bill emphasized that they needed the island in just two days from then. The concierge responded, "This may be a little difficult, but for a price, I'm sure I can find you a nice place that will meet your needs." Bill explained, "This is our honeymoon. We'll pay what we need to pay. Get us the best deal you can." The concierge answered, "But of course. I always do the best I can for my customers. You can count on me." Bill told Mary, "I'm sure he'll find us a nice place. The man seems highly motivated. I'm sure he knows he'll be rewarded for good service. He knows this area like the back of his hand." Mary sighed, "We can enjoy our meal now. No more need to worry about privacy or finding a suitable island."

The food came and they eagerly enjoyed the meal. The prime rib was excellent and the shrimp were delicious. Even the water tasted good. Mary looked fondly into her new husband's eyes. She loved being married to him. He was an interesting man. She knew she would never grow bored with him around. Mary asked, "What kinds of things should we do here in Australia, besides diving?" Bill stated, "They have many terrible fires here. I'd like us to call on their Department of Natural Resources and see if they have any plans to reduce the number of wildfires they are experiencing." Mary exclaimed, "That sounds interesting. What do you think we can do about wildfires?" Bill responded, "If they are open to the introduction of new tree species into this area, I'll recommend planting wide bands of red oak trees as fire barriers. The local flora contains too much highly flammable sap which feeds the wildfires. Red oaks are difficult to set fire to. They will grow in a wide variety of climates. I'll recommend that many species be experimented with in order to find some types of trees that will grow well here and be beneficial in reducing the frequency and intensity of wildfires. We have the same problem in the western United States. California is notorious for wildfires." Mary quipped, "Well, a prophet is never recognized in his own home town. Possibly they will listen to us here, even though such suggestions will probably not be listened to in the States. Everyone is so intent on protecting the original flora and fauna, they are blind to the need for prevention of devastating fires."

Bill and Mary talked for hours about forestry and the environment, as they enjoyed their meal and had some blueberry pie for dessert. After they were finished with the pie, they drove back to their bungalow. The concierge greeted them as they returned. He told them, "I have located a nice private island with only one bungalow on it. You can enjoy complete privacy. The price is only two thousand dollars. I'm sure you will agree it is a nice price for such short notice." Bill shook the man's hand, "It is indeed a good price. How soon can we move in?" The concierge responded, "It is available for you tomorrow noon. Shall I arrange transportation?" Bill stated, "That would be fine. We'll leave it up to you." He slipped a fifty dollar bill into the man's hand. The concierge smiled and stated, "I will have your transportation ready whenever you decide to leave."

Bill and Mary retired to their bungalow and enjoyed the roomy sauna together. They had spent a full day with the flight and walking on the beach. It wasn't long before they grew drowsy and climbed into their king sized bed. Mary and Bill prayed together before they went to sleep. Mary prayed, "Forgive my sins Lord Jesus. Thank you for our prosperity and for bringing Bill and I together. Help us to know how to put our money to good use, so it will help the poor and also help the environment. You have given us the earth to enjoy. We want to be good stewards and help keep the earth green with plenty of trees. Please protect us and my dad. Watch over dad's friends as they try to develop businesses that will be good for the environment." Bill prayed, "Forgive me my sins Jesus my Lord and Savior. Help me to be a good husband to Mary. Protect us from harm and give us wisdom in how to use our money. Thank you for this island paradise and all the beautiful fish and corals. Amen." They dreamed of the secluded island they would be going to the next day. It seemed almost too good to be true.

After sleeping in late, Bill and Mary had breakfast brought to their room. They had a leisurely breakfast. Bill said, "I'm glad we packed light. Since we each only have two suitcases, it won't be difficult to move from here to the island." Mary agreed, "Yes, packing light is the way to go." They finished the breakfast of eggs and bacon, and called the concierge to let him know they were ready to go to the island. In just a few minutes he appeared with two porters, who carried the suitcases to the waiting limo. Bill and Mary were driven to the marina where a cruiser was waiting for them. In just ninety minutes they were pulling up to the pier in front of their island bungalow. The cruiser's crew eagerly moved the suit cases into the bungalow. Bill tipped them generously and reminded them to come back in seven days. The crew left silently.

There was an ice box in the bungalow which Bill had been assured would be refilled with food and drink on a daily basis. The boat would bring supplies at noon each day. The food was included with the price of the one week stay. One of Cairn's foremost chefs would be helping to prepare the food. The refrigerator was full of soda pop, water and fruit drinks. The concierge had made certain that one bottle of their favorite wine was in the ice box, as well. He was a terribly thoughtful and clever man. Bill thought for a moment about how beneficial it is to tip the concierge well. There were warm blankets on the bed, which would come in handy for the beach. Mary pulled their snorkel's and fins out of the largest suit case. She insisted, "Let's get in the water while the sun is still high in the sky. The colors will be most brilliant right now." They donned their suits and headed for the water's edge with their fins and snorkels in hand.

It didn't require much swimming to get out to a nice shallow reef with many beautiful fish to watch. There were trigger fish, orange and white striped anemone fish, and the ever present angel fish. The varieties were too numerous to mention. From fluorescent orange to ice cold blues, pinks, reds, whites, there was every color in the rainbow present in these fish. Bill and Mary were careful not to disturb any of the sea creatures. They weren't well enough versed in what was poisonous and what was not, to start touching things. That isn't necessary anyway. Better to just observe and not disturb things.

It was a relief that no sharks were present. Visitors to the island were asked not to throw food in the water. It would throw off the delicate balance of nature in the area. With no garbage in the water, there was little to attract sharks. They liked deeper water. Here the water was only fifteen to twenty feet deep.

Because they were snorkeling, Bill and Mary had to work harder. They constantly needed to swim back to the surface for air. In about thirty minutes they started to tire and contented themselves with slowly swimming along the surface facing down towards the bottom. This was pleasant, but it didn't afford as many close encounters with the fish. It was nice though, to see the many different types and colors of coral. At one point they had a good view of a manta ray swimming by along the ocean bottom. After about an hour of this sort of leisurely snorkeling, they decided to sun bath for awhile. It was two in the afternoon and the sun wasn't quite as hot as it had been at noon. They spread out one of their blankets and then gently applied sun screen to each other. Bill had placed a bucket full of ice and fruit drinks beside the blanket. Everything was set for a nice relaxing afternoon in the sun. In spite of the sunscreen, they both got a little bit sunburned. They had fallen asleep in the sun and didn't wake up till six in the evening. The bungalow came supplied with a modest nightly allotment of firewood. Bill prepared the wood for the evening fire. He didn't light it till dark. Once the sun had set, they started the fire and had sandwiches by the fire. They spread out their blanket close to the fire and enjoyed the intimacies of married life with the warmth of the fire soothing them. It was a wonderful beginning for their official honeymoon.

Far from their warm fire another fire was burning. It was the eternal fire of hell. Satan once again had grown bored and called on his old friend Nostradamus to pass the time with him in dialogue.

Satan: It bothers me to see Mary Thresher living such a blessed existence. I can't stand that thought of her getting away with double crossing me. She is so pure and happy. I can't stand it. I must intervene.

Nostradamus: Is it worth risking the loss of your dental chair. Ruth, the angel, may prohibit you from getting another one. She is certain to take the one you have if you attack Mary Thresher.

Satan: Once again, you speak with great clarity and wisdom, good friend Nostradamus. I must make Mary's punishment look like something she has brought on herself. Today she has been over exerting herself, has she not? All that snorkeling, the sunbathing robbed precious salt from her body in the form of sweat. Now she is exerting herself powerfully with her husband. Wouldn't it seem only logical that she would develop a muscle cramp while diving tomorrow? Just when she is at the deepest depth of her dive, I'll cause a sever cramp in both of her legs. That should do her in. How can the angel trace it to me?

Nostradamus: It sounds like a good plan. I have no experience with how sensitive angels are. Ruth is probably busy with many projects. It seems likely that you can get away with this. You must make the final decision.

Satan: I'm certain you are right about Ruth. Anyone that powerful must have many important duties. How can she watch me every minute? God cannot stand to watch me. My evil deeds repulse him. That is why he leaves watching me to Ruth. As long as I just tempt people, she doesn't interfere. If I could only temp Mary in some serious manner, I wouldn't need to risk losing my dental chair at all. What might work with her?

Nostradamus: She might be tempted by power. What sort of power do you think she would go for?

Satan: Let's try making her desperate for money. We'll send someone in to tempt her with a stock tip that seems too good to pass up. She naturally liked blackjack. She won't be able to pass up a sure way to double her money on the stock market. She'll never suspect that it's a scam. She's still young and naïve and so is her husband. They want to be independent and show off to Jim how they can increase their wealth. I'm certain this will work. Once she's out of money, she'll crave power. She'll go to the casinos. She won't even realize she is praying to me for good luck. I will blind her to that. Then she will be open to my attacks, and I won't need to worry about God defending her through his angel, Ruth.

Nostradamus: Wealthy Christians can afford to stay pure in heart. Take away all their wealth and watch them blow on the dice for good luck. Watch them us any psychic power available to them to know when to bet big. They know that God doesn't play cards. Who do they think is helping them know when to bet big?

Satan: Precisely. I feel certain things will unfold just as I have predicted. Mary will call on me rather than beg her father for more money. She has never had to live poor. It won't suit her at all.

Nostradamus: She is a fair weather friend. She goes where the good life is. If she thinks Ruth, the angel, has deserted her, she'll call on you. It is almost a certainty. Few things are absolutely certain. This is what I would call a high probability.

Satan: High probability is good enough for me. I'm going to go for it. I can't stand to see Mary Thresher enjoying life so much.

After Mary and Bill had enjoyed their week on the secluded island, they rented a house near the beach. After their first week in their new home, the concierge gave them Bill a call. He advised Bill that he had a hot stock tip for him. He said, "This stock will certainly double in just a few months. They've come up with a generator that will double the amount of electricity which can be generated by wind power. The generator operates with less resistance and can make much more efficient use of the available wind. It's the only generator of its kind on the market. I'm helping you because you are a generous tipper. I'm putting as much of my own money into this as I possibly can. I'll put you in direct touch with my broker. You'll get receipts for everything and a low broker's fee."

Bill took down the broker's phone number and told Mary about the deal. Mary was a little worried at first, but Bill said, "Think of how much more we could do for the poor and for the environment if we doubled our money in just a few short months." Mary stated, "It sounds like a great idea. I just don't know whether we should invest everything." Bill explained, "The more we invest, the more profit we will make." Finally Mary gave in. They wired all their money to the stock broker who had been recommended by the concierge. A month later they saw on the evening news that the stock investment had been a scam. They had lost all their money. Mary asked Bill, "What can we do now? We can't stay in this country with no jobs and no money. We can't fly home. We have no money for the plane tickets."

Bill stated, "We still have next months rent money. I say we go to the casino and try to win at blackjack. We're both good at the game. With the two thousand we have from the rent we can make enough money for our plane tickets home at least." Mary acquiesced, "I've got to admit, I don't see any other way out. I really don't want to go begging to my dad for money, right after he gave us each a billion dollars! That would be truly humiliating."

Bill took the money out of the safe and they dressed casual for the casino. Bill picked a dealer he felt comfortable with and started playing blackjack. Mary took half of the money and chose a different dealer. They played for several hours and managed to double their money. Mary played some slot machines and quickly hit the jackpot on one of them. It paid out twenty thousand dollars. Mary went to the high stakes blackjack table and doubled her money again. She was becoming addicted to gambling. Mary whispered to Bill, "I think I'm a little too lucky. I'm enjoying this too much." Bill laughed, "Do you think old Satan is trying to win you back?" Mary frowned, "Don't laugh. I'm serious. No one wins this much. I think Satan is up to something." Mary whispered, "Satan made us lose all our money and now he's trying to make us feel obliged to him." Mary cashed in all their chips and went out to the car. Bill followed. Mary said, "Drive out into the country. We need to find a nice place to pray. Bill drove as rapidly as he could. When they reached the countryside there were some run down houses which attracted Mary's attention. She said, "Let's pull up to that house and see if anyone's home." Bill drove up to the door. Mary got out and rushed up to the door and knocked vigorously. An elderly woman came out an asked what she wanted. Mary said, "I know this sounds unusual, but we want to get rid of some money. We won it at the casino and now we don't want casino money." The elderly woman smiled. "You came to the right place. Money is money here. I sure could use some. My roof is leaking and I haven't been able to get any money for years. My husband died five years ago and had no money to leave me. I was just about to go to the trustee for some food money." Mary handed over the money in a paper bag. "Be sure to help some other people too. It always feels good to help others."

Bill and Mary returned to their house. "Now what do we do?" asked Mary. Bill said, "I guess we use our original two thousand dollars to pay the rent." Suddenly the room became white with bright light. Ruth appeared out of nowhere. She smiled at Mary and said, "You did the right thing by giving away the casino money. Satan caused you to lose your two billion dollars. He also caused you to win at the casino. He was trying to tempt you. You have pleased God by not giving into him. I have spoken to your father about these things. He is wiring each of you another billion dollars, with the demand that there shall be no more playing the stock market. You are to leave that to him. He wants you to receive more training in investment before you start taking big risks. He would prefer that you follow your love of forestry." Mary exclaimed, "This is more than I could have ever dreamed of. We've learned our lesson. No more high risk stocks." Bill stated, "I've learned my lesson. We'll be contented to promote tree planting and dive along the Great Barrier Reef. That should keep us occupied for awhile."

"That sounds good." replied Ruth. "Now if you'll excuse me, I need to go visit Satan and talk about the fine line between Satanic attack and temptation. We think he's getting a little too pushy. I may have to make his dull dental drilling machine disappear for awhile." Ruth disappeared.

Ruth suddenly appeared in hell just as Satan was waxing his dental chair. Satan gasped as Ruth started to point her sword at the chair. Satan screamed, "Please! I'll never even try to tempt Mary and Bill again. I'm done with them. Please! Not the chair! Ruth paused and smiled. There is a way that you can keep your chair. We'll be sending down some big time bankers who sell mortgages at exorbitant interest rates. Be sure to drill them first, before anyone else. Understood?" Satan smiled, "Always eager to work on that type of banker. I've got one question for you, though. Do any bankers make it to heaven?" Ruth replied, "Some make it because of the infinite grace of God, but it certainly isn't because they actually deserve it. There's a place reserved for them in the lowest reaches of heaven. They can almost smell the sulfur from your hell, there." Ruth disappeared and Satan set about preparing his drilling machine for the first banker.

## The End

CPSIA information can be obtained
at www.ICGtesting.com
Printed in the USA
LVHW092134150819
627864LV00001B/146/P